There Goes the Bride

Also by M. C. Beaton

There Goes the Bride

An Agatha Raisin Mystery

M. C. BEATON

MINOTAUR BOOKS

NEW YORK

THERE GOES THE BRIDE. Copyright © 2009 by M. C. Beaton. All rights reserved. Printed in the United States of America. For information, address St. Martin's Press, 175 Fifth Avenue, New York, N.Y. 10010.

www.minotaurbooks.com

Library of Congress Cataloging-in-Publication Data

Beaton, M. C.
    There goes the bride : an Agatha Raisin mystery / M.C. Beaton. —1st ed.
        p. cm.
    ISBN 978-0-312-38700-6
    1. Raisin, Agatha (Fictitious character)—Fiction.   2. Women private
investigators—Fiction.   3. Brides—Crimes against—Fiction.   4. Cotswold
Hills (England)—Fiction.   I. Title.
    PR6053.H4535T46 2009
    823'.914—dc22

                                                            2009016578

First Edition: October 2009

10   9   8   7   6   5   4   3   2   1

This book is dedicated with love to my husband,

Harry Scott Gibbons

There Goes the Bride

Chapter One

ONE OF AGATHA Raisin's greatest character defects was that she was highly competitive.

Her former employee, young Toni Gilmour, had set up her own detective agency, financed by another of Agatha's ex-detectives, Harry Beam. Agatha worked around the clock, taking on every case for her own detective agency she could in order to prove that the mature could beat the young hands-down.

Then there was the awful business about her ex-husband, James Lacey, planning to marry a beautiful woman. Agatha had persuaded herself that she no longer had any feelings for James because she had fallen for a Frenchman,

Sylvan Dubois, whom she had met at James's engagement party.

But stressed out and overworked, she had taken a tumble down the stairs of her cottage, cracking three ribs and severely bruising one buttock.

Urged by everyone to take a break, she decided to go to Paris after finding Sylvan's phone number through the Internet. They would stroll the boulevards together and love would blossom. But when she phoned him, he sounded distant and then she heard a young female voice call out in English, "Come back to bed, darling."

Blushing, and furious with herself, Agatha found her old obsession with James Lacey surfacing again. It was like some disease, gone for long stretches, but always recurring.

Agatha remembered that James had accused her of never having listened to him. He worked as a travel writer but had said that he planned to write a series of guidebooks to famous battlefields. Dreaming of surprising him with her knowledge of his subject, Agatha decided to visit the site of the Charge of the Light Brigade in the Crimea and so take that holiday everyone was telling her she needed badly.

She would go first to Istanbul and take it from there. She had stayed in Istanbul before, at the Pera Palace Hotel, made famous by Agatha Christie in her book *Murder on the Orient Express,* but settled on booking a room at a hotel on the other side of the Golden Horn in the Sultan Ahmet district, under the shadow of the Blue Mosque.

The Artifes Hotel was comfortable and the staff were friendly. Agatha, although tired after the flight, felt restless. She peered in the mirror and saw the ravages of her competitiveness clearly for the first time. She had lost weight and there were dark shadows under her eyes.

She left her suitcase unopened and wandered out of the hotel. There was an interesting café close by, the Marmara Café. She peered in. The walls were lined with carpets. At the end of the long café was a vine-covered terrace.

But the tables on the terrace seemed full. Agatha hesitated.

A man rose to his feet and said in English, "I'll be leaving shortly."

Agatha sat down opposite him with a sigh of relief. She saw to her delight that there was an ashtray on the table and pulled out her cigarettes.

"Are you English?" she asked her new companion.

"No, I am Turkish-Cypriot. My name is Erol Fehim."

Agatha assessed him. He was a small neat man wearing a good jacket. He had glasses and grey hair. He exuded an air of innocence and kindness. Agatha was immediately reminded of her friend, the vicar's wife, Mrs. Bloxby.

She introduced herself in turn and then ordered an apple tea.

"What brings you to Istanbul?" asked Erol.

Agatha explained she was stopping off at the Artifes Hotel until she worked out a way to get to Balaclava in the Crimea. "I'm staying at the same hotel," said Erol. "We could ask there."

Lonely Agatha warmed to the sound of that "we."

It transpired there was a weekend shopping cruise from the Crimea returning to Balaclava on the following day. The helpful Erol said he would go with her to the shipping office. It took them ages back on the other side of the Golden Horn to find it. Agatha was grateful for Erol's company because nobody spoke English. She booked a double cabin, not wanting to share with anyone.

Back at the hotel, the ever-obliging Erol told her he was busy that evening but he would take her along to the ship early the following afternoon and see her off.

Agatha phoned her friend Sir Charles Fraith. "Where are you?" he asked.

"In Istanbul."

"Great city, Aggie, but you're supposed to be taking a rest. Wouldn't a beach holiday have been better?"

"I don't like beach holidays. I've met a nice man."

"Aha!"

"He's really very kind. Reminds me of Mrs. Bloxby."

"Aha!"

"Aha, what?" demanded Agatha crossly.

"He must be a very normal, decent man."

"He is."

"I thought so. If he had been unattainable or mad, bad and dangerous to know, you'd have fallen for him."

"You think you know me but you don't!" snapped Agatha and rang off.

In the taxi on the road to the boat the next day, Agatha asked Erol about himself, but she barely listened as he explained he owned a small publishing company. In her mind, Agatha was already leaning on the rail of a white cruise ship while a handsome man stood beside her and looked into her eyes as the moon rose over the Black Sea.

The ship was a shock. It was a Russian rust bucket. In vain did they search for another ship; Agatha's ticket was only valid for the tramp steamer.

"It's all right," Agatha said to Erol. "It'll get me there. Thanks for all your help."

She was assisted by the crew over piles of goods. The decks were blocked with cargo. As she stumbled down to her cabin, she noticed that even the fire exits were also blocked with cargo.

Then Agatha realized to her horror that in her haste she had forgotten to say goodbye to Erol or get his card. She dashed back up on deck but Erol had gone.

The other few passengers were Ukrainian women, and the crew were all Russian. None spoke English. Soup was all Agatha could eat at dinner. The ship had not moved. She retired to her cabin and read herself to sleep.

When she awoke in the morning, the ship was still at the port. At last it set sail. At first it was bearable as she was able to stand on a tiny bit of the deck that was free of cargo and watch the palaces on the Bosphorus slip past, but once the boat reached the Black Sea and there was nothing but water to look at for miles, Agatha retired to her cabin, wondering whether she would survive the journey. She had booked a hotel, the Dakkar Resort Hotel in Balaclava, on the Internet before she left the hotel in Istanbul, and had asked for a taxi to meet her on arrival.

Two days later, when Agatha felt she could not bear another bowl of soup—the only thing she found edible—and shuddered at the prospect of another visit to the smelly toilets, the ship finally arrived.

As she struggled through customs with the Ukrainian women and their massive shopping—some had even bought mattresses—she saw to her relief a taxi was waiting with a driver holding her name up.

Oh, the blessings of a civilized hotel with a smiling beautiful receptionist and a well-appointed room. The receptionist said, "I was horrified when you e-mailed us about arriving on that boat. It's the *Gervoisevajtopolya,* famous for being awful. I didn't think you would make it here in one piece."

Agatha showered and changed. She then went down to the reception and asked the one who had welcomed her to arrange a guide and interpreter for the following day to take her to the site of the Charge of the Light Brigade.

But the next day proved to be a waste of time. In vain did she insist she wanted to see the site of the Charge, which had taken place during the Crimean War on twenty-fifth October 1854, where 118 were killed and 127 wounded. In vain did she take out her notebook and say she wanted to get to the valley between the Fedyukhar Heights and the Causeway Heights.

The pretty young translator, Svetlana, persevered with the guide, but he took Agatha to one Soviet World War II memorial after another, all in the Russian Communist style, with muscular young men pointing in all directions, while even more muscular women gazed balefully at some unseen enemy.

The sympathetic Svetlana said she would arrange for her tour bus to pick up Agatha the following morning. And so eventually Agatha found herself on the battlefield. But it was a plain covered in vineyards. No skeletons of horses, no abandoned guns, it stretched out mild and innocent under the sun, as if the most famous cavalry charge in history had never taken place.

Agatha returned wearily to the hotel. Her favourite receptionist gave her a welcoming smile. "We have two English guests who have just arrived," she said. "They might be company for you. A Mr. Lacey and a Miss Bross-Tilkington."

He'll think I'm stalking him, thought Agatha. Of all the rotten coincidences! "Get me my bill," she said. "I'm leaving now. And don't tell these English visitors about me. How the hell do I get out of here?"

"You can get a plane from Simferopol Airport."

"Call me a cab!"

James Lacey wandered over to the window of his hotel room. His fiancée, Felicity, was asleep. He was feeling some twinges of unease. What he loved about Felicity was the way she looked at him with her large eyes, appearing to drink in every word.

But on the plane journey, when he was enthusiastically describing the cavalry charge, he felt Felicity shift restlessly in her seat. For the first time, he wondered if she were listening to him. "The order to charge was given," said James, "and a spaceship landed in the valley and some little green men got out."

"Fascinating," breathed Felicity.

"You weren't listening!"

"Just tired, darling. What were you saying?"

James heard a commotion down below the hotel. He opened the window and leaned out. A woman had tripped and fallen getting into a cab. He only got a glimpse but he was suddenly sure the woman was Agatha. A familiar voice rose on the Crimean air, "Snakes and bastards!"

James ran down the stairs and out of the hotel, but the

cab had gone. He took out his mobile and phoned his friend, Detective Sergeant Bill Wong, back in the Cotswolds.

"Bill, " said James, "did Agatha say anything about being upset by my engagement?"

"No," said Bill. "I honestly don't think she was."

"But she was just here in Balaclava. Agatha has no interest in military history. I hope she isn't chasing after me."

Bill was also a loyal friend of Agatha's. "Just a coincidence," he said. "You must be mistaken."

James re-entered the hotel and asked the receptionist if a lady called Agatha Raisin had just checked out. The receptionist said firmly she could not give out the names of other guests.

Agatha decided on returning to Istanbul to take that much-needed holiday and forced herself to relax. She visited several of the famous sites: Ayasofya, the Blue Mosque, the Spice Market where James Bond got blown up in *From Russia With Love,* and the Dolmabache Palace on the Bosphorous. At the end of a week, she phoned her friend Mrs. Bloxby. After telling Agatha the village news, Mrs. Bloxby said, "James called round looking for you just after you left. He's got a contract to write a series of guidebooks on battlefields. He was just off to the Ukraine and after that, Gallipoli. How is Istanbul?"

"Great. Eating lots and reading lots."

When Agatha rang off, she took out her BlackBerry and Googled Gallipoli. The site of the disastrous Allied landings by the New Zealand and Australian and British forces in 1915 was in Turkey!

Should she go? Commonsense told her to leave it alone. Fantasy conjured up an image of dazzling James with her knowledge. He wouldn't know she had been in the Crimea. She could backdate her visit and say she had been there the year before. So, you see, James, I really am interested in military history. You never really knew me.

Agatha thought briefly of phoning up the Dakkar Resort Hotel to see if James was still there, but decided that he must be. He had a lot of research and writing to do.

Agatha managed to find a taxi driver who spoke English. The Allied landings had taken place all the way down the Gallipoli Peninsula, so she settled on ANZAC Beach, site of the Australian and New Zealand troop landings to the north of the peninsula, by the Aegean Sea. The taxi driver assured her it was only a few hours' trip from Istanbul.

The rain was drumming down by the time she reached the famous beach. She took photographs, she read the moving dedication on a monument to the fallen soldiers of both sides, and then wearily got into the cab thinking dismally that she should have stayed in Istanbul and just read up on the place.

Her taxi was just moving back out onto the main road again when a car with James at the wheel and Felicity beside him passed her. She ducked down, to the surprise of her driver.

Bill Wong got another phone call from James that evening. "I'm telling you, Bill, I saw her at Gallipoli. She's chasing me! Please find out if she's all right. I'm afraid she's taking my engagement badly."

Long afterwards, Agatha was to blame her visit to the two famous battlefields as having been caused by that fall down the stairs. She must have hit her head. How could she have been so stupid?

For back in the familiar surroundings of her cottage in the village of Carsely in the Cotswolds, back to work, Agatha's obsession with James faded away.

She comforted herself with the thought that James had surely not seen her, and besides, she had told everyone that her holiday had been spent entirely in Istanbul.

Shortly after her arrival home, on a pleasant Saturday afternoon, she decided to visit Mrs. Bloxby at the vicarage.

The vicar's wife welcomed her. "I know you probably want to smoke, Mrs. Raisin, but it's quite chilly in the garden." Both of them belonged to the Carsely Ladies' Society, where the members addressed one another by their second names, and despite their close friendship, the two women found the custom impossible to break.

"I'll live without one," sighed Agatha. "Rotten nanny state. Do you know that pubs are closing down at the rate of twenty-eight a week?"

"The Red Lion is in trouble," said Mrs. Bloxby.

"Never! Our village pub?"

"We're all trying to rally round, but an awful lot of drinkers don't want to go to a place where they can't smoke. John Fletcher didn't think it would strike so hard."

"He's got quite a big car park at the back," said Agatha. "He could put up one of those marquee things with heaters."

"He hasn't the money for that now."

"Then we'd better start raising some," said Agatha.

"If anyone can do it, you can." Agatha's past career was that of a successful public relations executive.

"Are you going to Mr. Lacey's wedding?" asked Mrs. Bloxby.

"Of course. They're being married in Felicity's home village of Downboys in Sussex. I suppose they'll arrange accommodation for us all."

"I asked about that," said Mrs. Bloxby. "We're expected to make our own bookings. There's the town of Hewes not too far away."

"Cheapskates! I hope I can still get a room."

"I think you have one. Toni Gilmour has been invited and knowing you were away and the possible shortage of rooms, she booked a double at The Jolly Farmer in Hewes."

The doorbell rang and Mrs. Bloxby went to answer it. She came back followed by Bill Wong. Bill was half Chinese and half English. He had a strong Gloucester accent and the only thing oriental about him was his rather beautiful almond-shaped eyes.

"Hullo, Agatha," said Bill. "Thought I might find you here. You've been putting the frighteners in your ex."

"I don't know what you're talking about," said Agatha, turning red. "How are your parents?"

But Bill was not to be deflected. "James phoned me from the Crimea. Told me he saw you. Then when he went to Gallipoli, there you were again. He thinks you're stalking him."

"The vanity of men never ceases to amaze me," said Agatha.

"But what on earth were you doing?" asked Bill.

"It's coincidence, that's all," said Agatha. "I was on holiday. I was James's wife, remember, so I learned a lot about military history."

"Oh, really? When was the Battle of Waterloo?"

"Mr. Wong," said Mrs. Bloxby gently. "You are surely off duty and not interrogating a suspect. Tea or coffee?"

"Coffee, please."

When she had served coffee, Mrs. Bloxby broke the heavy silence between Agatha and Bill by asking Agatha how she would go about fund-raising to save the village pub.

Anxious to escape any further questions from Bill, Agatha began to talk of running an initial campaign in the local papers and then holding a fete to raise money. "Maybe I'll get a smoking celebrity," she said.

Bill eventually left and drove into police headquarters in Mircester to start his shift.

He decided to phone James, who was staying with his future in-laws in Downboys in Sussex.

"I spoke to Agatha today, James," said Bill. "I don't know what she was doing at the battlefields, but Agatha likes to compete with people. You'd better watch. Maybe she plans to turn out her own guides. No, I shouldn't think for a moment she was stalking you."

Detective Sergeant Collins listened outside Bill's door. She was jealous of Bill and highly ambitious, so she often listened to his calls, hoping to steal a march on him. But Bill's call this time seemed to be nothing important. Only some chat about that infuriating Raisin female.

The days before the wedding seemed, to Agatha, to hurtle past and soon she was in Toni's car being driven to Sussex. Agatha had agreed to let Toni pick her up in Mircester and drive her because her hip was hurting again. A surgeon had told her that she really must begin to think seriously about having a hip operation.

Toni was wearing a leather jacket over a black T-shirt. A broad leather belt was slung low over her slim hips and her black trousers were tucked into a pair of pixie boots. Her fair hair was cut short and layered.

Agatha glanced at her sideways and sighed. Her own figure, although she had lost weight, seemed to sag even more these days. She had been neglecting her exercises. Sometimes early fifties felt young enough to her, but on days like this, seated next to the glowing youth of Toni and going to her ex's marriage to a gorgeous girl made her feel ancient. Agatha's legs were still good and her brown hair thick and glossy.

The countryside sped past. "Half a league, half a league, half a league onwards," muttered Agatha.

"Oh, we got that at school," said Toni. *The Charge of the Light Brigade.*"

Agatha winced. She had forgotten where the quotation came from.

"What's in your enormous suitcase?" asked Toni. "We'll only be there for a couple of days."

"Because I don't know what to wear," said Agatha, "so I brought as much as I could. I don't know whether to be dressy or smart casual."

"They'll all be wearing hats like the Duchess of Cornwall," said Toni.

"I haven't got a hat."

"Neither have I. You always look smart."

"How's business going?"

"We're actually beginning to make a profit."

Agatha fought down a surge of competition. Just look where that character defect had got her. Making a right fool of herself. At least she could try to keep clear of James.

Toni hit that idea on the head by saying, "There's some sort of pre-wedding party tonight at Downboys."

"Why?" moaned Agatha. "The groom's not supposed to see the bride before the wedding."

"I don't think that bothers people these days," said Toni.

"Why did you book us in at a pub? Doesn't Hewes boast a hotel?"

"It has two. But they've been taken over by Felicity's relatives and friends. I think their accommodation is being paid for. Maybe James didn't know he was expected to pay for his side of the church. The pub, The Jolly Farmer's pretty reasonable."

"I hope that doesn't mean a communal bathroom."

"No, bathroom en suite promised."

"I thought you might have wanted to travel down with Harry Beam," said Agatha.

"He's following us down. As we're sharing a room, it's better if we turn up together," said Toni.

.   .   .

Hewes was an attractive old market town situated by a river. The pub turned out to be a sort of pub/cum/hotel built round an old courtyard.

Their room was large and pleasant with a low-beamed ceiling, flowery wallpaper and two comfortable beds. There was even a desk with a plug for Internet access.

"What time is this party?" asked Agatha.

"It's at eight o'clock this evening. Buffet supper thrown in, so we don't need to bother about food."

"How did you find all this out?" asked Agatha.

"I phoned up for directions and found out about the buffet supper."

"I wonder if James hoped I wouldn't attend," fretted Agatha. "I've a good mind not to go."

"Don't leave me on my own," said Toni.

"I thought that by this time you wouldn't be afraid of anything," said Agatha.

"Not when I'm working," said Toni. "But the English middle classes frighten me when I have to meet them socially. I feel they can see right into my council estate soul."

Toni had hardly any time to get a shower and change. Agatha monopolized the bathroom and then covered her bed in dresses and trouser suits, worrying over what to wear.

At last she settled for a blue-and-gold evening jacket with a short black velvet skirt and high heels.

Toni was wearing a short white chiffon dress and gold leather high-heeled sandals.

Agatha felt a pang of envy. Oh, to be young and wrinkle-free again!

Both were nervous when they set out—Toni hoping she did not make some social gaffe or other and Agatha dreading that James would confront her over her visits to the battlefields.

"I'll lie!" she said out loud.

"About what?" asked Toni.

"Never mind."

The village of Downboys was built around a crossroads. In the centre was an old pub, a church and a small grocery store. It seemed a very gloomy sort of place. Although the evening sky above was still cloudless after a sunny day, the trunks of the trees were black with damp.

"Let me see," muttered Toni, squinting down at a piece of paper on her lap. "I turn left at the crossroads, then a few yards and make a right into a cul-de-sac and their house is the villa at the end. I can hear music. They must have hired a band. This is it. Damn! The drive's crammed with cars. "We'd better park here and get out and walk."

They walked up the drive towards the sound of the jaunty music. "Isn't it still usual to have a stag party for the man the night before and a hen party for the women?" grumbled Agatha.

"I thought it was," said Toni.

The Bross-Tilkingtons' villa was large and Victorian. The front door was standing open. They walked in. A young man wearing nothing more than a bow tie and a leather apron asked them for their invitations.

"I didn't know this was fancy dress," said Agatha.

"I'm from Naked Servants," the young man said, smiling. He studied their invitations and then said, "Go through the house and out through the French windows. The party is in the marquee on the lawn."

"God, how naff!" muttered Agatha. "Am I getting old, Toni? That vision didn't rouse a single hormone."

"Cheered me up," said Toni. "I'm more at home with vulgar people. And a semi-naked servant is definitely vulgar."

Agatha hesitated. "Maybe I'll go back to the pub and drive back later and pick you up."

"Not like you," said Toni, taking her arm. "Let's face the music."

They walked out through the French windows towards a huge striped marquee on the lawn.

There was another nearly naked young man at the entrance. He took their cards and bawled out their names but his voice was lost in the sounds of a medley from *Mary Poppins* being belted out by a brass band.

"Food and tables," said Agatha. "Let's grab something to eat and drink and sit down."

"Don't you want to circulate?"

"No."

"I see Bill Wong over there. I'm going to talk to him," said Toni, "and then I'll join you."

Agatha decided to have a drink first. She ordered a gin and tonic and then carried her glass to a table in a corner and sat down. She was soon joined by the members of her detective agency staff—Phil Marshall, Patrick Mulligan and Mrs. Freedman.

Phil was in his seventies, Patrick, early sixties, as was Mrs. Freedman. Agatha, in her early fifties, instead of being glad of their company, felt obscurely aged by it, especially when the crowd of milling guests parted to show her the beautiful bride-to-be standing with her arm linked in James's.

And then James saw her. He whispered something to Felicity and made his way to Agatha's table.

"I'd like a word with you," he said.

"Sit down," said Agatha, trying to smile but feeling as if her face had been Botoxed.

"In private—outside. Can't hear myself think for that band."

Agatha was about to protest, but at that moment the band launched into the music from *The Guns of Navarone*. She rose and reluctantly followed him outside.

He looked the same as ever, thought Agatha miserably—tall and handsome with his blue eyes and his thick hair going a little grey at the temples.

"I can't think of a more polite way of putting it," said James. "But were you stalking me?"

"I don't know what you mean," said Agatha defiantly.

"Well, let me spell it out for you. I went all the way to Balaclava and saw you fleeing the hotel. Then I went to the ANZAC landings—and guess what? You were just leaving there as well. Were you chasing me?"

Agatha opened her mouth to lie, to give a furious denial, but then she thought, what does it all matter anymore? He's getting married.

"You upset me at that engagement party of yours when you said I had never listened to you. I wanted to prove you wrong. I had a holiday due to me. I'd taken a tumble down the stairs and I think that must have addled my wits. I was going to stun you with my military knowledge."

James began to laugh. Then he said, "Oh, Agatha, you are an original. Let's take a stroll and talk about something else. You're looking very well. How are things at—? Oh, what is it?"

One of the nearly naked young men had materialized beside them. "Mr. Lacey," he said, "your fiancée wishes to speak to you."

"All right. Tell her I'll be with her in a moment."

"Whose idea was it to hire the Naked Servants?" asked Agatha.

"Felicity thought it would be fun."

"And you were happy with that?"

"Agatha, don't needle me. I'll tell you this," said James with sudden passion, "if I could think of a way to get out of this bloody forthcoming marriage, I would."

"Shoot her?"

"Don't be flippant. Stop creeping around us!" The latter to a Naked Servant who had appeared beside James and was avidly listening.

"I only came to tell you that Miss Felicity is wondering where you are," said the young man huffily.

"I'm coming," said James wearily.

Agatha sadly watched him go.

Chapter Two

AGATHA RETURNED TO her table. Charles, with Mr. and Mrs. Bloxby, came up to join her, followed by Harry, Toni and Bill Wong, and Agatha's ex-employee, Roy Silver.

They put several tables together to form a sort of Cotswold party. The band was taking a break and so they were able to talk.

"Mr. and Mrs. Bross-Tilkington look such an ordinary staid couple," said Mrs. Bloxby. "I must admit the Naked Servants shocked me."

"It was Felicity's idea," said Agatha.

"Oh, dear," said Bill. "I wonder what James thinks of it all."

"There's worse to come," said Toni.

"Like what?" asked Agatha.

"At the end of the party they have a competition where we vote for the handsomest servant. Then that servant is raffled off."

"You mean, pimped off," said Agatha.

"No, the winner of the raffle gets to sit on the Naked Servant's lap. Nothing more than that."

The vicar, Alf Bloxby, got to his feet. "We're leaving," he said.

Mrs. Bloxby didn't protest. "It's not really my scene, Mrs. Raisin."

"Nor mine either," said Agatha. "But I don't want to drag Toni away."

"Oh, you can drag me away anytime you like," said Toni. "Doesn't Felicity have any young friends? I mean, there's about five people her age and the rest are wrinklies and they all seem to be leering at the servants. It's creepy."

Agatha hesitated. "Apart from a few of James's friends and his sister, the rest of us here are his side of the church, so to speak. If we all get up and walk out, it'll look rude. Then we should really thank our hosts and we can't all march up to them together."

The Bloxbys sat down again. "You're right," said Mrs. Bloxby. "I wish something would happen to end this party."

24

Harry and Toni glanced at each other and then Harry said, "Toni and I are just going out for a bit of fresh air."

Just after Toni and Harry had left, Agatha found herself suddenly confronted by a furious Felicity. "You leave James alone," she shouted. "I know you've been stalking him. You're obsessed with him. Stay away from him!"

There was a shocked silence. "You can't say that one's beautiful when she's angry," said Charles. "She looked snake-like."

"Any ideas?" asked Toni when they were outside.

"We could cut the guy ropes."

"Might cause accidents if the marquee collapsed and smothered people."

"Let's walk round the tent and see if we can think of something."

They walked around the back of the marquee. The lawn ended in a small river.

"Look at that!" said Toni. "Over to the left."

Harry looked and saw kennels with a fenced-off yard. Behind the fence prowled four Alsatians.

"If they got out," said Toni, "I bet they'd head straight for the food."

"What if they savage the guests?"

"I'm sure they've been trained to only attack when ordered to. What do you think?"

They walked up to the kennels. "They do look hungry," said Harry. "Mind you, I could just lift this latch on the gate and let it swing open."

"There's a shed nearby," said Toni. "Let's make sure there isn't a kennel man."

They peered through the open door of the shed. A thick-set man lay asleep with an empty bottle of whisky behind him. A pot of boiling water with horsemeat in it stood on the stove. "He's forgotten to feed them," said Harry, turning off the gas on the cooker.

"What on earth are the Bross-Tilkingtons doing with four Alsatians?"

"They seem to be pretty rich. People get nervous these days." Harry took out a handkerchief and lifted the latch. "My dad had an Alsatian once. They're really all right. Stand back! All they'll want is food."

The gate swung open. The dogs sniffed. The evening air was full of the smells of food.

The four dogs moved slowly out of the kennels. Then, moving as one dog, they leaped forward.

"Poor James looks as if he wants to die," said Bill Wong as a roll of drums heralded the start of the raffle.

Felicity's mother, Olivia, walked up to a microphone in front of the band. She was a square-built sort of woman draped in peach silk. Her hair was so white and so rigidly lacquered it looked like a steel helmet.

"Now, ladies," she began. "The moment you have all been waiting for." Beside her, with cheesy grins on their faces, stood five Naked Servants.

And then the dogs erupted into the tent. One jumped on the buffet table while the others scrabbled to join it, finally pulling down the white tablecloth and sending plates of food flying. Guests were screaming and fleeing from the tent. Felicity's father was shouting for someone called Jerry.

Outside the tent, the guests were making rapidly for their cars and soon the night air was full of the sound of revving engines.

Agatha found Toni at her elbow. "Let's get out of here," said Toni breathlessly.

"You didn't, did you?"

"Don't ask. Just get in the car," said Toni.

"What I don't understand," said Agatha when she and Toni were lying in their beds later that night, "is why James let things get so far?"

"Maybe because he and Felicity were travelling a lot. He maybe didn't know just how awful his future in-laws would prove to be," said Toni, stifling a yawn. "I mean, those Alsatians! You'd think a good burglar alarm system would be enough."

"I wish tomorrow were over," moaned Agatha. "I wish I had a hat to hide under. I might nip out early tomorrow and see if I can buy one. Where's this church, anyway?"

"It's called Saint Botolph's," said Toni sleepily. "Right in the centre of the village. We can't miss it. I saw it when we were driving to the party."

"James doesn't want to get married now," said Agatha. "He told me."

"Then why doesn't he just do a runner?" asked Toni.

"He's in too deep," said Agatha miserably. "I could kill that girl."

Toni awoke next morning. There was a note on her pillow. "Gone hat hunting. If I'm late, don't worry. I'll take a cab to the church. Agatha."

Agatha had done a lot for Toni. She had rescued her from a drunken home and had found her a flat and a car. So Toni felt slightly guilty at enjoying being free of Agatha's often domineering presence for a short time at least.

She washed and changed into a straw-coloured raw-silk suit. Toni glanced at the clock. No sign of Agatha. She didn't want to be late getting to the church. She had found out last night that there hadn't been a field set aside for the parking and because she was wearing very high-heeled sandals, she wanted to get as near the church as possible.

At last she decided to leave. She met Bill Wong, who was staying at The Jolly Farmer as well.

"Where's Agatha?" he asked.

"Gone to buy a hat. She said not to wait for her. She's taking a cab."

"Is she bearing up? I think she's hating all this."

"No, she's fine."

"Had you anything to do with letting those dogs out?" demanded Bill.

"Me? No, of course not. You're not on duty now, Bill."

"Those dogs could have savaged someone."

"But they didn't, did they?"

"No," said Bill. "Some sort of kennel man appeared and took them off."

Outside the pub, Toni said hurriedly, "I've got to dash. I hope Agatha makes it on time."

It was a warm spring day with only a few fleecy clouds on a pale blue sky. But despite the warmth of the day, the old church was cold and damp inside. Toni joined the Cotswold contingent, answering muttered demands as to where Agatha had got to.

James appeared from the vestry with his best man, an

old army friend, Tim Harrant. The vicar took his place. The organ played softly.

"I'll go out and see if I can find Agatha," whispered Roy, who was wearing a white suit and a white Panama hat.

"He looks like the man from Del Monte about to say 'yes,'" muttered Harry.

The organ played on. The congregation shifted restlessly. There was a new arrival, but it was only the family's French friend, Sylvan Dubois.

Suddenly Roy appeared, shouting from the church entrance, "She's coming!"

The organ music died away and the church was suddenly filled with the strains of "You'll Never Walk Alone."

Heads twisted round and then turned back in disappointment as only Agatha Raisin walked in, wearing a peculiar sort of toque embellished with pheasant's feathers.

She and Roy squeezed into the pew next to Toni. "What's happening?" hissed Agatha. "Where's the bride?"

"Don't know," said Bill. He turned and looked at the entrance. "Here comes trouble. Toni, if you had anything to do with letting those dogs out, you're in for it now."

Alarmed, Toni watched as a plain-clothes officer, followed by several policemen, walked up the aisle. The detective bent his head over Olivia Bross-Tilkington and said something. Her sudden shriek rose up to the hammer-beam ceiling.

Then the detective faced the congregation. "Miss Bross-Tilkington has met with an accident," he said. "I want you to give your names to police officers, but do not leave the area until we tell you, and hold yourselves ready for questioning."

The vicar was trying to console Olivia Bross-Tilkington. Her frantic eyes raked the congregation, settling on Agatha, who had taken off her hat.

"That's her!" she screamed. "Murderess! You killed my daughter!"

She burst into noisy tears and was led off into the vestry by the vicar.

A table was carried to the entrance. Three policemen sat down behind it and began to take names and addresses as people began to leave.

Agatha slowly approached the table and started to give her name and address but only got as far as Agatha Raisin.

"Go back into the church and sit down until we are ready for you, Mrs. Raisin," said the policeman.

Dazed, Agatha went back and slumped down in a pew. What on earth had happened?

· · ·

Agatha's friends waited in the pub lounge bar for news. Bill Wong had said he would stay behind and find out what had happened.

The vicar, Mr. Bloxby, said impatiently, "Trust Mrs. Raisin to get us into a mess."

"It's got nothing to do with her," protested Toni. "She was out buying a hat."

Bill Wong came in. "Felicity's been shot," he said.

There was a general cry of dismay.

"So where's Agatha?" asked Roy.

"She won't be long."

"Who on earth could possibly have shot Felicity?" asked Toni.

"Need to wait for the police to get some ideas," said Bill.

"Isn't someone going to buy a drink?" asked Charles. "I could do with one."

"That's very kind of you," said Roy. "Mine's a vodka and Red Bull."

"I didn't mean me," said Charles. "There are too many of you."

"We'll each buy our own," said Bill. He signalled to the barmaid. After he had given his own order, he went outside and phoned Mircester police headquarters on his mobile phone and explained that he might have to stay on for another day. He wanted to go back to the police station, but had been firmly sent away and told it was not his territory.

· · ·

At Mircester police headquarters, Detective Inspector Wilkes said to Detective Sergeant Collins, "You take over the burglaries on the south side."

"What's happened to Wong?"

Wilkes told her.

Collins's eyes gleamed with malice. "That Raisin female probably did it."

"Why?"

"I happened to be passing Bill's room and overheard him protesting that Agatha had not been stalking her ex-husband. But he would say that anyway, being a friend of hers. Now there's a motive for murder."

"Well, while we wait for more news, Collins, go about your duties, which, I may add, does not include listening in to other people's private conversations."

After two hours had passed and Agatha still had not put in an appearance, Bill Wong could not bear it any longer and left them to see if he could find out anything more.

"It's a good thing it's a Saturday," commented Toni. "We've got detective agencies to run. We've all got to be back by Monday."

The day dragged on. They all went through to the pub dining room for dinner, with the exception of Patrick

Mulligan. He was a retired policeman and said maybe he could get someone at the station to tell him what was happening to Agatha. In the past, he had proved amazing at getting the police to open up to him.

After dinner, they wearily went back to the bar. Just when they were all about to retire to bed, Patrick reappeared, looking grim.

"They're holding Agatha and James for questioning," he said.

"Why?" demanded Charles. "Surely they must know neither of them could have done it."

Patrick shook his head. "They've decided they might have been in it together. They're waiting for the full results of the autopsy. But they think it was a bullet from a gun fired through the window. The window was wide open and there's a big tree outside. They figure someone climbed up that tree and shot her.

"Her father said that Felicity was in her wedding gown. She had gone up to her room to make sure her make-up was okay. He heard a shot but evidently people are always shooting rabbits and things in the woods round here, and Felicity's room is at the back of the house."

"What about the bridesmaids? Surely they heard something," said Roy.

"They had gone ahead to the church. Dad gets impatient and goes up to see what's keeping his daughter and finds her dead."

"That Frenchman," said Charles. "He was late getting to the church."

"Sylvan Dubois? He's got a cast-iron alibi. About the time they figure she was being killed, he was filling up his car at a garage just outside Downboys and he's recorded on the CCTV camera as clear as day. He drives a bright red Jaguar. Plenty of people noticed it on the road from the garage to the church."

"But couldn't he have filled up the car, gone and killed Felicity and then appeared in the church?" asked Toni.

"He was seen hurrying from his car straight to the church," said Patrick. "No one saw him anywhere near the house."

"They can't hold James," said Mrs. Bloxby. "His best man was surely with him all morning."

"Ah, this is where it gets worse. He was seen walking and talking with Agatha in Downboys very early this morning."

Charles half-rose. "I'd better get along there and make sure Agatha has a lawyer."

"Her lawyer's arriving tomorrow and she's now refused to answer any more questions until he gets here. One of those wretched Naked Servants gave damning evidence that he overheard James saying he wished he could get out of the wedding, to which Agatha suggested, 'Shoot her?' "

A groan went up. Toni turned to Harry. "I'm staying down here as long as it takes to get Agatha out of that police station." She turned to Patrick. "If they're still keeping her tomorrow, you'd better go back with Phil and Mrs. Freedman to keep things going. I hate the Bross-Tilkingtons," she said passionately. "I hate their stupid vulgar gossiping Naked Servants. What sort of people keep four Alsatians around?"

Roy shifted uneasily in his seat. He owed his present position as a public relations officer for a City firm due to the training and help he had got from Agatha when he used to work for her. Agatha had grown tired of the public relations business, and before setting up her own detective agency had sold up in London to take early retirement. "I've got a big account," he said. "I can't stay after tomorrow."

"Oh, piss off then, you wanker," snapped Toni, her carefully elocuted vowels slipping back into her former local accent.

"Well, I never." Roy got to his feet and stalked off.

"We're all upset," said Mrs. Bloxby. "There is nothing more we can do tonight. Let's all go to bed."

But Roy came back flanked by two detectives. One approached them and said, "I am Detective Chief Inspector Boase. This is Detective Sergeant Falcon. This is a very serious case. The Bross-Tilkingtons are much respected in this area. We need to take statements from all of you. The owner of this pub has said we may use his office." He consulted a list. "Miss Toni Gilmour?"

Toni stood up. "Come with us."

Toni followed them into the pub office, a small room furnished with a metal desk, two plastic chairs, three filing cabinets, and a large safe. On the wall behind the desk was a badly executed picture of the Sussex Downs.

Boase was a tall man with a sagging grey face, grey hair and weak, watery eyes. Falcon was smaller and plump with black hair and surprising large blue eyes.

"Now, Miss Gilmour," began Falcon, "what were your movements leading up to the wedding?"

Toni told him. Boase took out a cigarette and lit it and puffed a cloud of smoke up to fog the large NO SMOKING sign on the wall.

"Do you still have the note Mrs. Raisin left you?"

"I'm sure I have," said Toni.

"We'll get it from you later. Now, we have reason to believe that Mrs. Raisin was not happy about this marriage, that she is still obsessive about her ex-husband."

"I don't know of any reason to think that."

"Are you aware that Mrs. Raisin followed Mr. Lacey as far as the Ukraine and then Turkey?"

"No, I was not," said Toni, taken aback. Agatha had merely told her that she had gone on holiday to Turkey, but nothing about having seen James anywhere. "I certainly knew she had gone to Turkey on holiday, to Istanbul. But she had been there before and is fond of the city."

The questioning went on. How long had she worked for Agatha before setting up a detective agency of her own?

A tape recorder hummed on the desk. Toni began to feel really frightened for Agatha.

"Who would you say is Mrs. Raisin's closest friend?"

"We are all close friends," said Toni, "but I suppose you could say that Mrs. Bloxby is the closest."

"We'll have her in. Do not leave Hewes until we give you permission to do so."

As Mrs. Bloxby was told to go to the office, Toni sank down in a chair and said, "We'd better get out in the morning after the shops open and find out where she bought that hat and then see if we can trace her movements from there."

"Do they really want to waste time interviewing all of us?" asked Charles.

"Looks like it," said Toni. "I'm going to bed so I'll be fresh enough in the morning to do some detective work. Let's say we all meet for breakfast at eight o'clock—that's us detectives—me, Harry, Patrick and Phil. What about you, Charles?"

Charles smiled lazily. "I'm not a detective."

Toni thought that she had never been able to figure Sir Charles out. He was a beautifully tailored figure of a man with neat features and fair hair. He was as self-contained as a cat. He came and went in Agatha's life as he pleased. Bill had told Toni that he thought Charles and Agatha had once had an affair but Toni had never been able to see any signs of it.

Bill tossed and turned that night. When he had phoned his headquarters again to say that he should be back in Mircester by Monday, Wilkes had demanded to know why he had been overheard saying Mrs. Raisin had not been stalking her husband. Bill had described Agatha's visit to the two battlefields and said it was because Agatha was competitive and wanted to impress her ex with her military knowledge. The fact that James Lacey had been there around the same time was sheer coincidence. Now, he felt he had been disloyal to Agatha.

He wanted to stay on but had been told firmly by Boase that his help was not needed. As Bill had left the Hewes police station, he had seen Patrick deep in conversation with the desk sergeant. He had been going to approach him and then decided to leave Patrick to it.

They all met in the dining room in the morning. Toni had a copy of the Yellow Pages and was marking off all shops likely to sell hats.

The dining room door opened and a familiar voice said, "Pour me a cup of black coffee, someone. I'm knackered."

They all stared with a mixture of relief and amazement as none other but Agatha Raisin walked up to their table.

"Where's the hat?" asked Roy and then gave a nervous giggle as Agatha's bearlike eyes focused on him. "They're holding it as evidence," said Agatha. "Coffee, please. I wish I could have a cigarette. Stupid nanny state."

"So what happened?" asked Toni. "Did your lawyer get you out?"

"No, my stupid hat got me out. I bought it in Delia's Modes in the High Street. The salesgirl told me it was just like the one that the Duchess of Cornwall had worn for the French president's visit to Windsor."

"It certainly looked like roadkill," sniggered Roy.

"It looked all right in the shop," snapped Agatha. "Anyway, I still had time to go back to the pub and accompany Toni, but I wanted to be on my own to think. I got a cab out to Downboys and was going for a walk when I met James. We walked and talked. Then his best man came looking for him and they left for the church. I sat down on a bench. I wanted some more time to myself.

"Villagers passed me. A few stopped, looked at my hat, and asked, 'Aren't you going to the church?' The police had been doing a door-to-door in the village after the murder. So they collected evidence that I was where I said I was and the taxi driver confirmed taking me to Downboys. Of course all this took a long time to come in and they were reluctant to release their prime suspect."

A policeman appeared and said, "You all have to report to the police station to confirm your statements. You first, Mrs. Raisin."

"Has my lawyer arrived?"

"Yes, he is waiting for you."

The day dragged on with interview after interview. At last, they found they were all free to leave. "I wish I could have a word with James before we leave," Agatha fretted.

"Let it go," said Charles. "Just be glad you're off the hook."

Agatha and Toni went up to their room to pack. "I hate to quit like this," said Agatha. "Who on earth would want to kill Felicity?"

"This is one we have to leave to the police."

The phone rang. Agatha picked up the receiver. A voice strangled with tears said, "This is Olivia Bross-Tilkington."

"Look," said Agatha defensively, "I'm terribly sorry for your loss, but—"

"I'm sorry for what I said in church," said Olivia. "I want to hire you to find out who killed my daughter. I've been checking up on you."

"I don't have the resources of the Hewes police," said Agatha cautiously.

"But you have found out things in the past that the police could not. Please, Mrs. Raisin, come and stay as our guest."

"Is Mr. Lacey there?"

"He is leaving in the morning, which in the circumstances is the most unfeeling thing I have ever heard of."

Agatha made up her mind. "I'll be along in the morning."

She put down the receiver and turned to Toni, her eyes gleaming. "That was Olivia Bross-Tilkington. She's engaged me to find out who killed her daughter."

"Want me to stay with you?"

"No, Charles will do. He's helped me before. I'll just phone him." But Charles was not in his room and a call to reception informed Agatha that he had already left.

"I'll stay," said Toni. "For a bit anyway. You'll need an assistant. I'll run along and tell Harry to man the fort until I'm back, and you'd better get hold of Patrick and get him to take over your business."

As Agatha and Toni drove to Downboys the next day, the weather had broken and a miserable drizzle was oozing down from a grey sky.

"I'm not much looking forward to staying with them," said Toni.

"I was just thinking about that," said Agatha. "I might suggest we continue to stay at the pub and just turn up every day. We have to find out more about Felicity. Damn, James. I hope he hasn't left. Maybe he has some idea if she had any enemies."

The large electronic gates to the Bross-Tilkingtons' house were closed. Agatha groaned when she saw the press gathered outside.

"Reverse fast," she ordered Toni.

When they were once more outside the village, Agatha phoned Olivia Bross-Tilkington and asked if there was a back way into the property. Then she turned the phone over to Toni, who scribbled down instructions.

By approaching the village from a different angle, they found themselves outside a small lodge house where a man was waiting by the gates. He studied their car and then opened the gates.

"Odd, very odd," said Agatha as the car bumped up a narrow road leading to the back of the house. "Why all this security?"

"Yeah," said Toni. "I wonder if they were afraid of something even before the murder."

Chapter Three

GEORGE BROSS-TILKINGTON WAS waiting for them when they arrived. He was a heavyset man with a pugnacious tanned face under a thatch of thick grey hair.

"I don't want you here!" he said.

"But your wife—" began Agatha.

"I don't care what my wife says. Shove off!"

Olivia appeared behind him. "I invited Mrs. Raisin," she said. "I told you. She has the reputation of being a good detective *and I want to know who killed our daughter!*"

"The police—"

"I am not waiting for the local plods. Besides, Sylvan agrees with me."

"He what?"

"Talking about me?" Sylvan strolled into the hall. Agatha's heart beat a little faster. Then she remembered the humiliation of that phone call to Paris.

"I encouraged Olivia to call in the services of Agatha," he said.

"Why?"

"Why?" mocked Sylvan. "One would think you did not want the identity of the murderer to be discovered."

"Oh, do what you like," said George and stomped off.

"I'm so sorry about that," said Olivia. "Poor George is grieving and so he covers it up by getting angry." Her eyes were puffy with weeping. "First, I'll show you to your room. I was only expecting you, Mrs. Raisin."

"Call me Agatha. This is another detective, Toni Gilmour, who is going to assist me. But I think it would be better if we both continued to stay in Hewes. That way we can take a more objective view of things."

"Very well. Let's go into the lounge and discuss the matter."

Toni looked around the drawing room, or lounge, as Olivia had called it. It certainly looked more like a hotel lounge than a room in a private house. There were little islands made up of polished tables and tapestry-upholstered chairs embellished with gilt paint on the woodwork. There was no fire burning on the hearth. Instead the grate was decorated with orange crinkled paper. On a table by the

French windows stood a large vase of silk flowers. A polished yacht wheel emblazoned with the name CYNTHIA in gold letters hung over the fireplace. In one corner was a padded leather bar with glass shelves behind it full of all those odd bottles of drink that people usually collect on package holidays, and the shelves were illuminated with pink strip lighting.

Sylvan, Agatha, Toni and Olivia sat down round one of the tables. Toni took out her notebook.

"Why is there a ship's wheel over the fireplace?" asked Toni.

"That was my husband's first boat. Cynthia was his first wife."

"What happened to her?"

"She died of cancer."

Agatha was painfully aware of Sylvan Dubois. He was every bit as attractive as she remembered, with his thick fair hair going slightly grey, his hooded eyes and his slim figure.

"Now, about your daughter," said Agatha. "Did she have any enemies you can think of?"

"Everybody adored her."

"Had she been married?"

"No."

"But she was very beautiful," said Toni. "Surely she must have had a lot of offers."

"Of course."

"So was there a rejected man who might have wanted to kill her?" asked Agatha.

"It was the other way round," said Sylvan, his French accent light and mocking.

"What do you mean?" demanded Toni.

"She was what you call a dumpee."

"And what does that expression mean exactly?" demanded Agatha.

"It means she was engaged two times and two times the fellow called the engagement off."

"Sylvan," said Olivia, beginning to cry, "if you were not a friend of my husband's I would ask you to leave."

"How did you come to be a friend of James Lacey?" asked Agatha.

"I spilt some beer over him in a brasserie by accident. I apologized and we got talking. I gave him my card and said if he was ever in Paris again to look me up and I would buy him dinner. He did. I told him I was going to a friend's party and took him along. That was where he met Felicity."

Olivia dried her eyes. "It was love at first sight," she said.

"How do you know the Bross-Tilkingtons?" asked Toni.

"I was on holiday in Cannes. I met them there—oh—ten years ago and we've been friends ever since."

"What does Mr. Bross-Tilkington do for a living?" pursued Toni.

"George is retired," said Olivia. "He dealt in real estate. Foreign properties, mostly."

"In Spain?" asked Agatha.

"Yes, Spain and other countries."

"A lot of angry people have lost their homes in Spain. They've found out that the properties their flats were in had been built on agricultural land and after they had invested their life savings, the local Spanish council came along and bulldozed the buildings. A lot of them claim they had been tricked. The estate agents would say, 'Don't worry about a solicitor. We'll supply one.' And so they never found out about the danger until it was too late."

"None of that was going on when my George was selling houses," said Olivia angrily. "May I remind you it was my dear daughter who was killed?"

"I thought that maybe," said Agatha cautiously, "someone might have wanted revenge on the family by killing the daughter."

"Nonsense!"

"All right. Sylvan, are you sure that Felicity's two previous engagements were broken off by the men?"

"So I was led to believe."

"Have you their names and addresses?" Agatha asked Olivia.

"I'll get them for you." Olivia hurried out of the room. Then they all heard the doorbell and a voice saying, "We are sorry to trouble you, Mrs. Bross-Tilkington, but my forensic team would like another look at your daughter's room. And if you are up to it today, we have some more questions to ask you and your husband. Oh, don't leave, Mr. Dubois. You as well."

When Olivia and Sylvan had left the room, Agatha whispered to Toni, "Let's get out of here. See if that kennel man knows anything."

They went out through the French windows. The rain had stopped but the lawn was spongy under their feet.

"I hope he's got the dogs safely locked up," said Agatha uneasily.

"Yes, I can see them prowling about behind the fence," replied Toni as they drew nearer to the kennels.

"There's that little shed over there," said Agatha.

As they approached the shed, a small burly man came out and stared at them.

He wore a flat tweed cap, sports jacket, worn corduroy trousers and large battered black leather boots. His gnarled face had a squashed look, as if someone had put a heavy weight at some time on top of his head.

"What do you want?" he called.

Agatha approached him. "Just a word," she said. "Mrs. Bross-Tilkington has asked me to investigate her daughter's murder. Have you worked for the family long?"

"Five years."

"May I know your name?"

"Jerry Carton."

"I am Agatha Raisin and this is my assistant, Toni Gilmour. Can you suggest any reason why Felicity was murdered?"

"Dunno."

"Why is there all this security? I mean, state of the art burglar alarms, electronic gates and those Alsatians?"

Jerry spat in the direction of Agatha's feet. "It's a wicked world, lady."

"But not that wicked," put in Toni. "I mean, were you asked to be on your guard against any people in particular?"

"Why don't you take your questions and shove them up—"

"Now, now," admonished Agatha in her best Carsely Ladies' Society manner. "Ladies present."

"Oh, yeah. Where?"

"Come on," said Toni. "This moron doesn't know anything."

"Have you got a police record?" asked Agatha.

He took a menacing step towards her. "Get out of here or I'll turn the dogs loose."

"Let's go," said Toni urgently, tugging at Agatha's sleeve.

Agatha reluctantly walked back with her to the house. She took out her mobile phone and called Patrick.

"I'm still on the road back," said Patrick. "What's up?"

"Nothing," said Agatha. "I wondered if you could use your police contacts to find out if the kennel man here has a police record. His name is Jerry Carton."

"I'll try. Bill's in the car in front of me on the motorway. I'll follow him to Mircester and see if he'll look up the files."

Agatha thanked him and rang off.

She and Toni walked back into the drawing room. Toni looked around and sighed. "This is not what I expected of the middle classes."

"Just like any other class," said Agatha. "They come in all flavours and some of them are horrible."

"Did you read any Betjeman at school?"

Agatha thought of the violent comprehensive she had gone to, where most of the day was taken up fighting off bullies and trying to hear what teachers were saying above the racket made by the pupils in the classrooms.

"I hope you're not going to turn all intellectual on me," said Agatha. "I used to get a lot of that from James." James, she suddenly thought, where are you now?

"It's the poet John Betjeman. I remember reading a poem, 'The Subaltern's Love Song.' Betjeman had a crush on a girl called Joan Hunter Dunne. She died recently at the age of ninety-two."

"What on earth has that to do with anything?" grumbled Agatha.

"Well," said Toni, "you know what things were like in my home. I had a picture of the middle classes as portrayed in that poem: a picture of secure, solid homes, money, adoring parents welcoming suitable young men to take me to the club dance. But it's not like that at all."

"To be fair," said Agatha, "the sorts of people who get into trouble so that we have to go detecting are usually not very normal." Then she thought of some of James's friends and repressed a shudder. She had to admit to herself that she had taken early retirement and moved to the Cotswolds because she had been following a dream of classy security.

"There are good people around," she added. "Take Mrs. Bloxby. People like that."

Sylvan came into the room. "This is all very tiresome," he said. "Questions, questions, questions. And now I suppose you have more."

Agatha glanced at her watch. "Why don't I take you to lunch?"

"That would be fine. And your pretty assistant?"

Agatha glared at Toni, who said hurriedly, "Actually, if you don't mind I'd rather go back into the town to find out what I can there."

"We can walk down to the pub," said Sylvan. "I've eaten there before. The food's quite good."

.   .   .

The pub in the centre of Downboys was called The King Charles. A badly executed painting of Charles II swung in a rising wind outside the old inn. It was a Tudor building, whitewashed with black beams, bulging at the front with age.

"There's a free table just over there," said Sylvan, propelling her towards it.

"Do they take an order for drinks here or do I have to go to the bar and get it?"

"We get our drinks first and then a waitress will come round for our order."

"I'll get them," said Agatha. "My treat. What are you having?"

"A half of lager."

The bar was blocked by villagers. One man turned round on his bar stool and saw her. He whispered something to his companions and they all swivelled round.

"If you've had a good look," said Agatha, "then make way. I want to get my order in."

They shuffled off their bar stools and left a space for her. Suddenly everyone fell silent. The barman was a small fussy little man wearing a blazer, white shirt and cravat over grey flannels. His face was fake-tanned and his teeth cosmetically whitened. Agatha guessed—as it later turned out, correctly—that he was someone who had retired from show business to open a pub.

She ordered a gin and tonic for herself and a half of lager for Sylvan and walked back to the table.

A buzz of conversation rose again.

"Cheers," said Sylvan.

"Don't you ever speak French?" asked Agatha. When she had dreamed about him, he had always murmured to her in French.

"When I am speaking to a French person, yes—otherwise, why bother?" He handed her a menu. "The roast beef and Yorkshire pudding is very good," he said.

Agatha thought of her waistline, but she was very hungry, so she smiled and said she would try it.

Sylvan raised a hand. A waitress promptly appeared.

"What will be your pleasure, sir?"

"You, you gorgeous creature."

The waitress, who was thin and spotty, giggled with delight. As if aware that Agatha Raisin's eyes were boring into him, Sylvan gave the order. Agatha detested men who flirted with waitresses, or indeed anyone, whilst in her company.

"I'm glad of this opportunity to talk to you," she said.

He smiled. "And I am glad of that."

"For a start, you know George Bross-Tilkington. Why all the security?"

"It's become a dangerous world. He's a rich man. There were several burglaries in the village a few years ago. That's when he began to take precautions."

"And what of Felicity? I'll need to interview her two previous fiancés. Are you sure they broke off the engagements and not the other way around?"

"So I was told. Would you like some wine?"

Just a short time ago, Agatha would have said yes, hoping for a romantic lunch, but now she was in full detective mode. "No, thank you," she said. "I want to keep a clear head. So what was Felicity really like?"

"Very beautiful."

"I want to know about her character."

"I don't think she had much of a character. She worked so hard on her appearance—beauticians, hairdressers, personal trainer, all that."

"But James is an intelligent man. Surely beauty wasn't enough."

"Felicity had a special talent. Here's our food. I am very hungry. Let's leave the questioning for a little."

The roast beef was delicious. Agatha ate a bit but then she felt she simply could not wait to find out what Felicity's special talent had been.

"What talent?" she demanded.

"She was very good in bed."

Agatha slowly put down her knife and fork. "How do you know?"

He gave a very Gallic shrug and his eyes sparkled with amusement.

"You mean, you had her?"

Again that shrug. Oh, James, thought Agatha miserably, was I not good in bed?

"But that was surely not enough," she protested. "He told me he wanted out of the marriage."

"Ah, but he is an honourable man. The date was set, the ring was on the finger. He is much older than Felicity and runs on a different set of ethics. Now, if Felicity had changed her mind, she would have cancelled the wedding even at the last minute."

"Did she love him?"

"Felicity had so much self-love there was not room for anyone else."

"Bitch!" said Agatha. Her eyes filled with tears.

He leaned across the table and took her hand in a warm clasp. "You must care very deeply for your ex-husband."

"It's not that," said Agatha furiously. "Whatever I felt for James is long gone."

She could not explain that the whole business was making her feel old and frumpy. Also, she reminded herself that James had divorced her. No honour there. No sticking to the marriage vows.

"Eat your lunch," he said gently.

"I think I've had enough," said Agatha, pushing her plate away. "I should get back to the house."

"Have a coffee and brandy. You need it. Je t'en pris."

Agatha pulled herself together. Good detectives surely didn't emote all over the place. Patrick and Phil, for example, went doggedly on with their work. Bill Wong, even in the throes of a broken romance, never let emotion cloud his judgement. It was all to do with increasing age, she thought miserably. That awful feeling of losing powers of attraction, of growing wrinkles, nasty little face hairs, and a stomach that kept insisting on dropping slowly south were all very demoralizing. She must stop regarding Sylvan as a Frenchman she had thought attractive and stick rigorously to her job.

Toni meanwhile had secured the names and addresses of Felicity's ex-fiancés. The first one was Bertram Powell and he worked as a solicitor in Hewes.

His secretary, a plump young woman with lacquered hair and a power suit, asked if she had an appointment and when Toni said she hadn't one, the secretary gave a thin smile and said Mr. Powell was busy all that day.

Toni glanced at her watch. Lunchtime. No sound from the inner office. She thanked the secretary and left.

She began to check the restaurants near the solicitor's office, asking in each one for Mr. Powell. She struck lucky at a steak house in one of Hewes's cobbled lanes that led down to the river Frim. The maître d', assuming that Toni was joining Bertram Powell for lunch, escorted her to his table.

"Hello," said Toni, holding out her hand.

He rose from his seat, looking puzzled. He shook her hand. The maître d' held out a chair for Toni and she sank down into it.

"Who the hell are you?" demanded Bertram. He was much older than Toni had expected him to be. She thought he might be approaching fifty. His face was broad and pugnacious and his nose looked as if it had been broken at one time. His hair was black and sleek, as black as his small eyes.

"I am a private detective investigating the murder of Felicity Bross-Tilkington."

Bertram looked suddenly amused. "Go on with you. You're a child."

Toni handed over her card. "Don't be put off by appearances. I am very good at my job."

A waiter hovered with a menu. "Have you something uncomplicated, like steak and chips?" asked Toni.

"Of course."

Toni ordered a well-done steak and chips and a bottle of mineral water. "I do not expect you to pay for my lunch, Mr. Powell."

"I should hope not. I can't tell you anything about Felicity. We were engaged some time ago."

"Why did you break off the engagement? You were the one to end it, weren't you?"

"Yes."

"Why?"

"I'd rather not say."

The waiter brought Toni's steak. The speed with which it arrived was a bad sign, she thought. It had probably been sitting up on a hot plate in the kitchen for ages. The waiter was an extremely good-looking young man with slim hips. Bertram eyed him appreciatively as he walked away.

Toni's eyes sharpened and she studied Bertram's clothes. He was wearing a dark suit, striped shirt and silk tie, all suited to his job. The suit was exquisitely tailored.

"Why are you staring at me like that?" demanded Bertram.

"I was wondering whether you were gay," said Toni.

"You cheeky little . . . Oh, for heaven's sake, yes, if it does you any good."

"And that was why you broke off the engagement?"

"Yes, her father found out. I didn't know he'd put a private detective on to me."

"So why did you break off the engagement and not her?"

"She wanted to go through with it. She told her father that's what she wanted. I had only just discovered I was gay."

"But what about sex?"

"Felicity thought about little else. She pointed out that we had never had any trouble in that department and that the invitations to the wedding had all been sent out. But I insisted everything was off. George Bross-Tilkington was furious. The Bross-Tilkingtons, when you get to know them, are as common as muck. George's father, old Harry Bross, was a scrap merchant down the East End of London. Tilkington was his wife's maiden name. He relished the idea of being the sort of squire of Downboys with his daughter marrying a solicitor. He said a good psychiatrist would soon sort me out. I refused.

"So he spread it around the town that I was homosexual. I thought that was me finished, but it backfired on him because I began to get all the gay law cases in town. And we're near enough to Brighton, England's San Francisco. Don't mess with the Brosses, young lady. They're a scary bunch."

"Anything criminal?"

"Not that I know of. George seems to have made a legitimate pile of money out of the real estate business in Spain."

"Have you heard any rumours about why they have so much security at their home?"

"No. It's not unusual. Lots of crime around, and people with money get scared of burglars."

"When were you engaged to Felicity?"

"Eight years ago."

"And there was someone after you who called it off. Ernest Wheatsheaf. Do you know where I can find him?"

"At the Southern Bank in the High Street. He's the

bank manager." Bertram called for the bill. He asked for a separate receipt, paid his bill, and hurried off. Toni finished as much of her steak as she could, remembered to switch off the powerful tape recorder in her open handbag under the table, paid her bill and went out in search of the Southern Bank.

Sylvan watched Agatha from under his heavy-lidded eyes as she excused herself and went to the toilet to freshen up. She had a nice high bottom and very long legs, he thought appreciatively, and she exuded an air of very strong sensuality of which she seemed totally unaware. Perhaps a little fling might brighten up his visit. George had begged him to stay on.

At the bank, Toni demanded to see the manager, and was told that he was too busy and someone else would need to deal with her.

"That's a pity," said Toni. "I've just won the lottery and—"

"Oh, wait here," said the woman at the desk by the door. "I think he'll want to see you."

In three minutes' time, Toni was ushered into Ernest Wheatsheaf's imposing office. He was a tall thin man with greying hair. Like Bertram, Toni guessed he must be pushing fifty. Why had Felicity never gone for men her own age?

Ernest seized Toni's hand in a warm clasp. "It will be a pleasure to handle your affairs, Miss . . . ?"

"Gilmour." Toni handed over her card. He studied it, his eyebrows almost disappearing into his hairline. "I am actually a private detective hired by Mrs. Bross-Tilkington to find out who murdered her daughter."

"Then leave my office immediately! You got in here under false pretences."

"Look, Mr. Wheatsheaf," said Toni, "you may as well practice on me because I am sure you will soon be interviewed by the police."

He had half-risen to his feet. He sank back into his chair.

"Why?"

"You were engaged to Felicity. They'll want to make sure it was you who called off the wedding."

"But what has that to do with murder?"

"They'll be checking out everyone who might have had a grudge against Felicity."

"You are very young to be a detective."

Toni opened her briefcase and took out a file with newspaper cuttings. "Have a look at those," she said.

He flicked through the newspaper cuttings, reports of Toni's successes. Although they had been due in the main to the detective work of Agatha Raisin, Toni was prominently featured because she was the most photogenic.

"You seem to know your job, miss," said Ernest, "but I cannot see how this murder has anything to do with me."

"You seem to me an intelligent man and someone in an important position in this town," said Toni, giving him a charming smile. "It's not that the murder has anything to do with you—of course not—it's just that you knew Felicity and sometimes—quite often, in fact—the character of the person who has been murdered can give a clue as to the reason for the murder."

The weather outside was clearing up. A shaft of sunlight shone through the office window and gilded the fair cap of Toni's hair.

Ernest suddenly smiled. "I can only give you ten minutes but I will do my best. Did you know Felicity?"

"No, but her fiancé invited me to the wedding. She was very beautiful."

"She was quite plump and she had brown hair when I was engaged to her."

"When was that?"

"Let me see, about five years ago. She seemed fresh and innocent and eager to please. I thought she would make a very good wife."

"You weren't in love with her?"

"I found her very suitable," he said repressively. "A man in my position must be careful whom he weds."

"So what happened?"

"I found her too . . . er . . . demanding."

"You mean sex?"

He actually blushed.

"Well, yes. It struck me as not being very ladylike. She was furious when I broke off the engagement. In fact, her mother and father threatened me with all sorts of lawsuits. Then she went off with her parents to somewhere on the Continent. When she returned a long time after, I forget how long, she had transformed herself into a beauty."

Wondering whether Ernest might be gay as well as Bertram, Toni asked, "Are you married now?"

"Yes, indeed, and very happily."

"Can you think of anything to do with Felicity that might drive someone to murder her?"

He said drily, "Perhaps her present fiancé found that murder was the only way of getting out of the marriage."

"What about the Bross-Tilkingtons? Anything there?"

Ernest's secretary put her head round the door. "Mr. Barnstaple is complaining that you are keeping him waiting, sir."

"Show him in. Good day, Miss Gilmour. I really must get back to work."

An hour later, Toni and Agatha met up in their room at the pub. Toni had phoned Agatha, telling her it would be a good idea to come back and listen to the two taped interviews.

"It's all very odd," said Agatha, after she had heard the tapes. "I must talk to James."

"Are you going to phone him now?"

"No. I talked to Mrs. Bloxby this afternoon and she said he was back in Carsely. I want to talk to him face to face. I'll leave now and be back tomorrow. See what you can find out about Sylvan Dubois. That's an odd sort of friendship. Keep trying to get Olivia on her own. You shouldn't be too much troubled by the press. There's been a double murder over in Brighton, so most of them have hurried off there."

Back to the Cotswolds drove Agatha after picking up her car in Mircester, back down the leafy roads leading to Carsely. She was assailed with a sudden longing to forget about the whole thing. Her excellent cleaner, Doris Simpson, had been looking after her beloved cats in her absence. How wonderful it would be just to go to bed, have a long lie-in the morning, and spend a lazy day reading books and playing with her cats.

The old mellow stone houses of the village of Carsely glowed in the late-evening light. The weather was unusually warm and the little gardens were heavy with blossom.

She parked in front of her cottage and went in to a sulky reception from her cats. She patted them but they oiled away from her and stood expectantly in front of the garden door. She let them out, went upstairs and refreshed her make-up, and then walked next door and rang the bell.

James answered it. They stood looking at each other for a moment and then James said quietly, "Come in, Agatha."

Agatha walked into the familiar room and sank down on the sofa, biting back a yelp as her arthritic hip gave a nasty twinge.

James slumped down in his favourite armchair by the fireplace. "What a mess," he said.

"Why didn't you stay on?" asked Agatha.

"Because I had to get away from George and Olivia. At first they accused me of the murder and after I was cleared by the police, the atmosphere was still hellish."

"You could have booked in at The Jolly Farmer with us," said Agatha.

He said in a low voice, "I had to get away. You have no idea what a fool I feel."

"Well, Olivia has hired me to find out who killed her daughter and I'm going to do it, so I need some clue as to why someone would want to bump her off. What was she like?"

"Very beautiful, as you know. She seemed to adore me. I was flattered by the way she hung on my every word. It was only on that Ukraine trip that I began to slowly realize that when I was talking, she was usually thinking of something else."

"Toni interviewed her two ex-fiancés. The first said he broke off the engagement because he was gay, the second because he found her too sexually demanding."

"Now that's ridiculous. Felicity was in fact rather shy."

"But the gay chap said she was oversexed and Sylvan Dubois said she was hot stuff between the sheets."

There was a long silence while James stared at Agatha. "Are you sure about this?" he said at last.

"Three of them are surely right."

"Good heavens! She was old-fashioned *maidenly* towards me. Said we should wait until after we were married."

"James, in this day and age? Didn't you find that a bit odd?"

"I was dazzled by her appearance and she seemed so sweet and innocent. When she went for you at that party, I could hardly believe it. But I had already discovered that she was extremely stupid, on the cusp of being mentally retarded. I would guess she had received practically no education at all. I had already approached George and told him I did not think I would make a suitable husband and he threatened me with every lawsuit under the sun and said if I broke his daughter's heart, he would kill me."

"Let me think," said Agatha. "I gathered from your engagement party that Sylvan was a friend of yours, and yet he seems to be pretty close to Olivia and George. How did you meet him?"

"I met him by accident in a brasserie. He spilled beer over me. We began to chat and I found him very amusing. We became friends. Then the next time I was in Paris, he invited me to a party at his friend's apartment and it was there that I met Felicity."

"Could you have been set up?"

"Conspiracy theories, Agatha? I could simply have been polite to the girl and left. The whole mess was entirely my fault."

"When did you propose?"

"Two days after I first met her. I'm a silly old fool, but it all seemed so romantic—Paris and the most beautiful girl in the world on my arm. Don't glare at me like that, Agatha. You've made a fool of yourself in the past. What about the last one who turned out to be a murderer?"

"Charles has been gossiping."

"No, Bill Wong. He worries about you."

"Did you get any hint of a rejected lover anywhere?"

"Not even a whiff. I didn't even know about her previous engagements."

"Why don't you come back to Hewes with me," urged Agatha. "We could go detecting like we did before."

"I'm sorry, Agatha, I have a heavy writing schedule and I just want to forget about the whole thing."

Agatha got to her feet, her small eyes boring into him. "Well, I think you're a wimp," she yelled and stormed out.

Angry tears ran down her face as she let herself into her

cottage. It had been humiliating to hear her ex-husband burbling on about how beautiful Felicity had been and romantic Paris.

Then she sniffed the air. Cigarette smoke! And she hadn't lit up a cigarette since she got back.

She took out her mobile phone to call the police and backed towards the front door.

"Is that you, Aggie?" called a familiar voice from the kitchen.

Charles!

Agatha put away her phone and went into the kitchen, scrubbing at her eyes with a handkerchief as she went.

Charles was sitting at the kitchen table, smoking a cigarette from a packet of Bensons Agatha had left on the counter. He had the keys to Agatha's cottage and dropped in and out as he pleased. Agatha had once tried to stop him, but then realized that often she was lonely and Charles's company was better than none.

Charles looked at Agatha's red eyes. "Been calling on James?"

"Yes, pass me one of *my* cigarettes."

"So what did he say about Felicity?"

"She appears to have had the reputation, according to two previous fiancés, not to mention that Frenchman, of being a nymphomaniac. But surprise, surprise. No sex for James till after the wedding."

"She may have been a nymphomaniac, but I think she

was a narcissist as well. She wanted to star on her wedding day. She probably pictured herself in white and pearls going up the aisle. Do you mean to say she was turned down before because of too much sex? Hard to believe."

"Trust you to think so. The first fiancé was gay, and the second, I gather from Toni, a stuffy bank manager who thought it was all not very *naice*."

Charles leaned back in his chair and blew a lazy smoke ring up to the beamed ceiling. "I once knew this girl who was really hot stuff," he said. "Got herself a reputation around the county. After her last affair was ended and no ring on her finger, I met her at a party. She was a little bit drunk and she confided in me that according to any future man, she was going to be the complete virgin. And she did eventually get married. Men can be stuffier than you think, and the old ways still apply—why marry when you can get it all and more without any responsibility whatsoever?"

"But James is an intelligent man! Why did he leave things until it was too late? He said he'd discovered she was very stupid."

"Stupid as a fox, Aggie. She looked gorgeous. Very flattering to a man of James's age to have an adoring piece of arm candy. Maybe he wanted children. Felicity was well within the child-bearing age. The idea of a son or daughter to carry on the Lacey name maybe blinded him. You never would face up to it, you know, that for a man of James's age to still be a bachelor meant there was something wrong."

"He married me," Agatha pointed out.

"We all know you're unique. Tell me how he met Felicity?"

Agatha told him what she knew.

"He could have been set up. Do be careful of Sylvan."

"Why? Do you think he's the murderer?"

"No, but I think he's a lightweight philanderer."

"It takes one to know one, Charles."

He smiled. "Doesn't it just."

They sat in silence for a while. Then Agatha said, "I'd better get back there tomorrow, but I'll call on Mrs. Bloxby in the morning before I go."

"I'll come with you," said Charles. He stretched and yawned. "I'm off to bed. Have they found the gun?"

"Patrick says they found the bullet but not the gun. They estimate it came from a Smith & Wesson 686SSR. He says it's got a stainless-steel cylinder, L-shaped, and can shoot from twenty-five yards. I'm off to bed. You do treat my cottage like a hotel," said Agatha crossly.

"Admit it. You're glad of the company."

Chapter Four

MRS. BLOXBY WAS eager to hear their news when they called on her the following morning. When they had finished, she said, "But surely there must be a lot of forensic evidence. If someone climbed that tree, they must have left traces of fibres or hair on the bark."

"It's hard to know anything when one isn't a member of the police force," grumbled Agatha. "I'm going back down there today."

"Mr. Mulligan seems to be able to extract information," said Mrs. Bloxby. "Wouldn't it be better to send him back there?"

But Agatha felt that *she* was the one who had been employed to find the murderer and didn't want an employee to steal any of the glory. "He needs to run things in the office," she said. "I'll call in on him before I leave for Downboys. Anyway, it's hardly like one of those CSI programmes. It'll take them ages to get any forensics results out of the lab."

"Must have been someone who knew the family well," said Charles. "I mean, the murderer knew about the bedroom and about that tree. You said she hadn't been having any sex with James and she was a bit of a nympho, so she might have been getting it somewhere else, say, from a lover who was in the habit of nipping up that tree and into her bedroom window. What kind of tree is it?"

"It's an old cedar," said Agatha. "You could practically walk up it, and there's great concealment with all those heavy branches."

"If she was that good in bed," Charles pointed out, "someone could have become obsessed with her, someone her father wouldn't dream of letting her marry. She may have been the bicycle of the village."

"Sir Charles!" admonished Mrs. Bloxby.

"It's a good point." Agatha sighed. "I'd better get going. Coming with me, Charles?"

"Maybe I'll follow you down."

Patrick gloomily said that he didn't have much further news, although he had already phoned his contact in Hewes that morning. All he could say was that Jerry did not seem to have a criminal record and the police were combing the grounds and dredging the river.

"What river?" asked Agatha.

"The river Frim. It's at the boundary of the property. Bross keeps a boat there."

Agatha checked and found that Patrick and Phil seemed to be coping well and set off on the long journey to Downboys. She stopped on the way for a greasy breakfast, having not bothered to eat anything earlier. She phoned Toni and asked her to meet her at the pub at one o'clock.

Toni was in the pub lounge bar. She jumped up as Agatha came in and said, "I've lots of news. Did you find out anything?"

"Only the make of gun and that the cedar tree was ideal for concealment and also that forensics will take ages to find anything."

Toni's eyes gleamed. "But the scene of crimes operatives found lots and I'm not surprised. They found hairs and traces of fibres from different sets of clothing, beer cans and chewing gum."

"What! Have we got an amateur murderer?"

"No, we've got the village boys. I chatted up some of the local youth in the pub last night. It seems that dear Felicity was in the habit of doing a slow striptease with the lights on and the window open before she went to bed."

"But the dogs! All that security!"

"They laughed and said the dogs were pussycats and Jerry is such a drunk he often passes out and forgets to feed them. They take along dog biscuits and meat and things and they've made pets of the beasts. They said you can sneak in and up to the house from the river side. They stopped laughing when I told them that the police were collecting every bit of evidence from in and around that tree."

"Did they ever see anyone actually getting into her bedroom by the window?"

"One of them, Bert Trymp, a bit older than the others, said one night he was going to try because, to put it in his charming words, she must be gagging for it. It's too difficult to leap from the tree to the window, so he carried along a ladder one night and up he went while his mates watched from the tree. Felicity sees his head and shoulders rising above the window and screams the place down.

"Bert is arrested but when Felicity's nightly striptease starts to come out, Bross-Tilkington drops the charges fast, makes a donation to the police widows-and-orphans fund, and the striptease stops."

"When was this?"

"Two weeks before the wedding."

"Are the police questioning Bert?"

"I don't know. Gosh, if this comes out in the press, poor James is really going to look like a sucker. No wonder her father was desperate to get her married off."

"And what about Jerry? Why wasn't he fired?"

"I thought maybe you could find out something from Olivia Bross. I'm going to drop the Tilkington. Such a mouthful. Was James able to be any help?"

"Not in the slightest," said Agatha bitterly. "She played the virgin with him. No sex until after we're married. I just don't understand James at all."

"Beautiful people get away with a lot," said Toni, "and Felicity was so very beautiful."

Agatha fought back an irrational impulse to cry.

"Let's go and see Olivia," she said. "Are the press still around? Do we need to go the back way?"

"No, we can use the front. Only a couple of local fellows."

Agatha phoned Olivia as they were almost at the villa and told her to open the electronic gates. The rain was falling steadily as they arrived. Toni got out to phone on the intercom, ignoring the questions of two sodden reporters. The gates opened and they drove in. The reporters tried to follow but were shooed back by a policeman on duty outside.

Agatha fretted that the only real bits of investigation had come from Toni and Patrick. She was determined to take over the questioning of Olivia.

"I wonder who cleans this place," whispered Toni. "I mean, I'm sure Olivia can't clean it all herself."

I should have thought of that, Agatha's mind grumbled. But she saw a way of getting rid of Toni. "Why don't you leave Olivia to me," she said, "and go back into the village and ask around."

"Wouldn't it just be easier to ask Olivia who cleans for her?" said Toni reasonably. "Then I'll take off and question her."

"Oh, all right." Agatha rang the bell. Olivia answered the door herself. "Oh, do come in," she said eagerly. "Have you any news?"

"A few leads," said Agatha. "I would like to ask a few more questions."

"Let's go into the lounge."

"Before we do that, would you please give us the name of anyone who cleans for you?"

"I don't see how that can be of any help, but there are two women, Mrs. Fellows and Mrs. Dimity. They live together in a cottage called Strangeways behind the church."

"I'll be off then," said Toni. "Back later."

Olivia and Agatha went into the drawing room. "Would you like tea or something?" offered Olivia.

"No, thank you. I wanted to ask you about that business about the local boys climbing up that tree and watching Felicity as she got ready for bed."

"That was disgusting!" cried Olivia. "My poor innocent daughter."

"What I really want to know is why your man, Jerry, wasn't sacked after that. He's supposed to be protecting the house."

Olivia looked uncomfortable. "He's so loyal to my husband and he swore it would never happen again."

"Now, in the case of both of Felicity's previous engagements, it appears the first was broken off because the man found he was homosexual and the second, because the bank manager found Felicity's desire for lots of sex rather off-putting."

"That's disgusting and none of it is true. It was George, my husband, who declared they weren't suitable. Like me, he wanted only the best for Felicity. I can only assume that both men are so furious at being rejected that they are now making up stories."

Could Olivia really be so naive? wondered Agatha.

"Is your husband at home?" she asked.

"He has gone out in his boat with Sylvan. He said he needed to get away for a bit."

"Without you?"

"I'm hopeless. I get so dreadfully seasick."

Agatha experienced a rare feeling of claustrophobia. The room was overheated, the long windows were steamed up, and Olivia seemed to exude sentimental stickiness from every pore. Agatha reminded herself severely that the woman facing her had just lost her daughter.

"I think I'd like to have a word with this Bert Trymp. Is he in the village?"

"He works at the garage, but he's a coarse fellow and will say anything."

Agatha was glad to be outside again. The rain was slackening off. It wasn't all that cold and yet Olivia had the central heating blasting away. The more she thought about Olivia's lack of knowledge of her daughter's sex life, the more puzzled she became. George Bross seemed a very domineering sort of man. Perhaps Olivia was simply a doting mother who gladly accepted her husband's interpretation of things.

She drove the short distance to the garage. There was a small showroom to one side, displaying secondhand cars for sale. Behind the pumps was an office where customers paid for their petrol. There was no shop in the garage selling groceries. Possibly the grocery store directly opposite had protested at any such idea. She asked an elderly man who was cleaning up discarded rubbish where she could find Bert Trymp. "In the workshop," he replied. "Round the back."

Holding her umbrella over her head and sidestepping oily puddles, Agatha made her way round to the shed at the back.

She asked a man in dirty blue overalls if she could speak

to Bert Trymp. "Bert!" roared the man, making Agatha jump. A young man emerged from the shadows at the back of the shed. He had a face like a younger John Bull: wide mouth, stocky figure, beer gut. "You that detective?" he asked.

"That's me," said Agatha. "Is there anywhere we can talk privately?"

"Pub's open," said Bert hopefully.

"Bit early for drink, isn't it?" asked Agatha.

"That's why the pub'll be quiet-like."

"Okay, ask your boss for permission."

"Don't need to. Me da's the boss."

The pub was quiet, with only two hardened drinkers propping up the bar. Agatha ordered a tonic water for herself and a pint of real ale for Bert. They sat down at a table as far away from the bar as possible. After Bert had taken a huge mouthful of ale, Agatha asked him, "I believe you got into some trouble over Felicity."

"Well, that were her doing. Egging us all on, like."

"The place is well guarded. How was she to guess that you and some randy schoolboys were watching her undress?"

"There's undressing and there's undressing, know what I mean? Her was doing more of a striptease, like. Taking every little bit off slow as slow."

"She still may not have known she was being watched."

"Oh, yeah? Well, one night, her shouts out, 'Show's over, boys,' and pulls the curtains close. That's a come-on. I thought, I'll have her, that I will. So next night, I gets a ladder and climbs up. She screams and yells. We all run for it, but the police are round the next day. Then I gets a visit from old man Bross. He says if it ever happen again, he'll kill me, but he isn't going to charge me. I'm telling you, after that I kept real clear."

"Have you any idea at all who might have killed her?" asked Agatha.

He scratched his head of thick brown hair. "See, it's like this. Her was provo . . . pro . . ."

"Provocative?"

"That's the word. Right little prick teaser. Now, if her 'ad been found in the woods, like, strangled and raped and all, well, everyone would like, say, her'd been asking fer it. But shot! You'd best be asking around for folks with guns."

Meanwhile, Toni was sitting in the parlour of the cosy cottage belonging to Mrs. Fellows and Mrs. Dimity. Over cups of tea, she had learned that the pair were widows and had moved in together to pool expenses. Either they had always looked alike, or proximity and age had given them the appearance of sisters. Both looked to be in their late fifties, and they both had the same tightly permed grey hair, round comfortable figures, and small twinkling eyes.

"But we don't know who could have killed Miss Felicity, and that's a fact," said Mrs. Fellows, "unless it was that fiancé of hers."

"Mr. Lacey? Why him?" asked Toni.

The women looked at each other uneasily and then Mrs. Dimity said earnestly, "Well, seeing as how you're investigating for Mrs. Bross . . ."

"You just call her Mrs. Bross?"

"Her full name's such a mouthful. Like I was saying, on account of that Mr. Lacey there were lots of shouting and rows. When Mr. Lacey heard about them Naked Servants, he hit the roof and called Mrs. Bross vulgar. Mr. Bross tried to punch him but Mr. Lacey pushed him down into a chair and said he'd changed his mind and he didn't want to get married. Miss Felicity cried something awful. Mr. Bross threatened Mr. Lacey with breach of promise and everything else. At last Mr. Lacey said, tired-like, 'Don't cry, Felicity. I'll go through with it.' And Miss Felicity brightened up no end and starts talking about arrangements for the wedding with her mother. To my way of thinking, Miss Felicity was always a bit simple."

"Why all the tight security?" asked Toni.

"It's always been like that since they came here. But we know on the day of the wedding, them dogs were locked up and the gates were standing open, ready for the bride to be driven to church," said Mrs. Dimity. "After the local lads were caught spying on Miss Felicity, that's when Mr. Bross went raging to Jerry and said he wasn't doing his job right. But there were always burglar alarms all over the place and security lights."

"How did the boys get past the security?"

"They came in from the river," said Mrs. Fellows.

"Are there many boats on the river?"

"A few. Mr. Bross, he wanted to claim the part of the river at the bottom of his property as private property, but he couldn't get to do that because it's a sort of right of way for other boats going down to the coast."

"So on the day of the murder," said Toni eagerly, "someone could have come by boat and—"

Mrs. Fellows interrupted her. "No, no. Think about it. A man carrying a gun would have been seen walking up from the river and across the gardens in broad daylight and carrying a gun."

"Was Felicity maybe cheating on Mr. Lacey?" suggested Toni.

"Don't think she had the time, and that's a fact," said Mrs. Dimity. "Mrs. Bross said they were always travelling here and there. They hadn't been engaged that long. Mind you, during the winter, Mr. Lacey went off on his own for about six weeks and Felicity and her parents went to Spain."

"To do business?"

"No, just for a holiday, they said. Mind you, we had to keep on cleaning," said Mrs. Fellows. "Mrs. Bross said she didn't want to see a bit of dust when she got back. Wait a bit. I 'member Jerry went with them and some man came to look after the grounds and the dogs. What was his name, Ruby?"

Mrs. Ruby Dimity sat in thought. Then she said, "Got it. Sean was his name. Just Sean. Didn't learn any other name. Irish as the pigs of Derry, he was."

"What was he like?"

"Hard to tell. Kept himself to himself. Didn't even come up to the kitchen for a cup of tea. Tall chap. Young-ish. Well, young to us. Maybe about thirty. Brown hair, plain face, nothing special, but very fit. He'd walk those dogs for miles."

Although Toni persevered for a while with more questions, she couldn't get any more information out of them.

As she was leaving their cottage, her mobile rang. It was Agatha. "Find out anything?"

"A little bit," said Toni. "Where are you?"

"In the pub. Bert's just left."

"I'll join you."

"You first," said Agatha when Toni sat down beside her. Toni told her about Sean. Agatha brightened. "Well, at least that's someone new to pursue. We'll get back to Olivia and find out where he is, where they got him from. Anything else?"

"I'm afraid our two cleaning ladies think it might be James. They heard James having one hell of a row over the Naked Servants and saying he wanted out of the engagement and Bross tried to punch him and then threatened him. Felicity began to cry and James at last said he would go ahead with it."

"If the police haven't got that bit of information yet, they soon will," said Agatha gloomily.

"What about Bert?"

"Not much use, except that he said Felicity wasn't just undressing, she was actually well aware of her watchers and doing a striptease."

"Cow!"

"Exactly. She was the full moo, believe me. Let's get back to the house of horrors and see if we can get an address for Sean."

Olivia looked puzzled for a moment and then her face cleared. "Oh, Sean Fitzpatrick. I remember. He lives on his boat down at the marina in Hewes."

"What is the name of his boat?" asked Agatha.

"I can't remember."

"Where is the marina?"

"I'm not very good at directions. But anyone in Hewes will tell you."

"That's odd," said Agatha as they drove off.

"What's odd?" asked Toni.

"Well, the funeral should be soon, as soon as they release the body. But Olivia looked quite perky, considering her precious daughter is not long dead."

"Maybe she's just putting a brave face on it," said Toni. "Actually, she does look as if she's full of some sort of pills. She's probably on a heavy dose of antidepressants. No one's supposed to grieve these days. Let's find this Sean."

After asking in Hewes for directions to the marina, they found it at the foot of a long winding cobbled street. Various expensive-looking yachts bobbed at anchor along with smaller craft. There was a small stone jetty and on the shore were several trendy boutiques and cafés with tables outside where a few brave people crouched over cups of coffee in a blustery wind.

"There's an office on that jetty," said Agatha as they both got out of the car. "We'll try there."

In the office, a man who looked as if he were dressed for the part of a nautical extra in a film sat behind a desk. He wore what Agatha had seen advertised as "a genuine Greek fisherman's hat" on his head and a white Aran sweater over a tattersall shirt with a silk cravat tucked into the neckline. Although surely aware of them standing in front of him, he continued to write something on a pad.

Agatha waited a few minutes and then said crossly, "Okay, you've impressed us with the fact that you are a busy man. We've got it. We're suitably impressed. We want to ask you a few questions."

He looked up, feigning tolerant amusement, and tipped his chair back. He had a craggy face with deep pouches under his eyes. "Want a boat?"

"No," said Agatha. "Or rather, a particular boat. Sean Fitzpatrick's."

"What's he been up to now? Seduced your daughter?"

"We are private detectives. I am Agatha Raisin and this is Toni Gilmour. We have been hired by Mrs. Bross-Tilkington to investigate the murder of her daughter. Now, where do we find him?"

"Walk along to your left when you leave here. It's a cruiser called *Helena*."

"And I wonder who Helena was or is," said Agatha when they left the office.

"There it is," cried Toni, pointing. "That's one really powerful boat. Must have cost a fortune."

"Mr. Fitzpatrick!" called Agatha.

There was no movement from the boat.

"Aren't we supposed to shout 'ahoy'?" asked Toni.

"Can't do that. I'd feel like a prat. *Mr. Fitzpatrick!*"

"The wind's carrying your voice away," said Toni. "Why don't I nip on board? He might be asleep or something."

Agatha wanted to say that she was quite capable of nipping on board herself but her hip gave that awful twinge—the twinge that kept crying out for a hip-replacement operation.

"Go ahead," she said gruffly.

She watched enviously as Toni leapt onto the deck. Toni called loudly but the only thing that met her ears was the hum of the traffic from the town above the river and the screech of seagulls overhead.

Toni looked across at Agatha, who made impatient well-go-ahead signs. Toni tried the door of the cabin and found it unlocked. She made her way down the companionway past the head, past a table in an alcove with a marine chart spread on it and then into the cabin. It was empty. Toni was about to retreat when she realized a cruiser this size must have a bedroom.

She opened a door at the end of the cabin. Lying on the bed was the prone figure of a man, fully dressed. A hole, like a third eye, was in the middle of his forehead. The exit wound had soaked the pillow in blood.

Toni slowly backed away, her face white. Then she turned and ran up on deck, calling wildly to Agatha, "Call the police. Murder!"

A combination of the wind and a mocking seagull's cry drowned out Toni's words, but Agatha saw the girl's white face and picked her way gingerly along a narrow gang-plank which Toni had ignored.

"He's dead. Shot. Get the police," panted Toni. Agatha took out her mobile and began to dial.

"What are you ladies doing on Sean's boat?" a voice called.

Toni heard the voice but not the words. She looked across at the jetty and saw Sylvan Dubois. She started to call to him, but he jumped on the deck. "It's Sean Fitzpatrick, I think," said Toni. "He's dead. Shot."

"Are you sure?" asked Sylvan, making his way to the companionway.

"Don't go down there!" shouted Toni. "It's a crime scene."

"I need to make sure he is dead. Did you touch the body?"

Toni gave a shudder. "No."

"I'll just check."

Agatha rang off and asked angrily, "Where's he gone?"

"To look at the body."

"I'd better go and see what he's up to," said Agatha.

"The police have arrived," said Toni, waving frantically as two squad cars came racing along.

Sylvan reappeared and helped them back onto the jetty. "You shouldn't have gone in there," raged Agatha. "It's a crime scene."

"I know that now," he said with a shrug. "But I had to make sure."

Police poured out of their cars, headed by Detective Inspector Boase. Agatha explained quickly what they had found and why they had been looking for Sean. Boase barked out orders. Agatha, Toni and Sylvan were to be taken to the police station and held for interrogation. Their fingerprints were to be taken and their hands checked for gun residue. Agatha was furious.

They sat and waited in Hewes police station after their fingerprints had been taken and their hands checked for what seemed ages.

At last the detective inspector returned with Detective Sergeant Falcon. "You first, Mrs. Raisin."

Agatha had a sudden sharp longing for James or Charles or even Roy. Charles had said he would follow her down, but in his usual cavalier way, he had not put in an appearance. She belonged to a generation when men were supposed to handle difficult situations. She was surprised at herself. Had she not built up two successful businesses? She squared her tired shoulders and sat down in the interrogation room.

"Coffee?" asked Boase.

"Police coffee?"

"There's a Starbucks next door."

"Great. Black. May I smoke?"

"If you must."

Agatha lit up a cigarette and thanked the gods that this

nanny state had seen fit to leave the prisoners or about-to-be prisoners with some indulgences.

A policewoman came in shortly carrying a tray of cardboard containers of coffee. It *would* have to be a policewoman who was sent for coffee, thought Agatha. In fact, did one still call them policewomen, or was it policepersons or—

"Mrs. Raisin! If you have quite finished daydreaming," said Boase. "Interview with Mrs. Agatha Raisin in the presence of Detective Sergeant Falcon and Police Constable Hathey. Time fifteen-hundred thirty. Begin at the beginning and tell us why you went in search of Mr. Sean Fitzpatrick."

Agatha explained again that Olivia had asked her to investigate the murder. She had learned that Sean Fitzpatrick had taken over guarding the house and grounds while the Bross-Tilkingtons and their man, Jerry, were abroad. They were told he had a boat. On locating the boat and getting no reply to their shouts, Toni Gilmour went on board and returned shortly to say Sean had been murdered. Mr. Sylvan Dubois had come along and gone aboard to check that Sean was really dead. "And that's all," she ended defiantly.

But that was far from all. She was asked to explain all her movements from the time she got up in the morning to what she had been doing before she had called at the boat. She reluctantly gave up details of her interview with Bert Trymp and how Toni had found out from the cleaners about Sean. Then she had to go over it all again from the beginning until she snapped, "Am I being charged with anything?"

"No," said Boase. "You are simply helping us with our inquiries."

"Then I'm out of here."

"Do not leave the area. We will probably wish to speak to you again."

Agatha sat down in the reception area to wait for Toni. How on earth could James detach himself from a murder case which involved him so closely? She must see him again. He surely must have heard something or other. "What are you dreaming about?" asked Sylvan, joining her.

"I am not dreaming, I am thinking hard. You know the family. You're friends with them. Surely you've got some idea."

He spread his hands. "They seemed a nice English family. Very hospitable. I don't think George Bross liked Felicity much."

"What! His own daughter?"

"Ah, you see, Felicity wasn't his daughter. He got drunk one night and told me. Olivia had an affair once. He loves his wife. Strange, *hein*? That dumpy little woman with the iron hair? They could not have children so he elected to bring her up as their own. He was desperate to get her married off and out of his life."

"Had she done something so terrible?"

"Who knows? But she did try to please him and when she turned herself into a raving beauty, that seemed to work for a while."

"Do the police know this?"

"I don't think so, and don't tell them."

"Who was the father?"

"You'll need to ask Olivia that. But do tell her you did not get the news from me. What about dinner tonight?"

Agatha would normally have leaped at the chance of dinner with this attractive Frenchman, despite the fact that she was still suspicious of him, had she not still been so shaken over this second murder. "Another time," she said gruffly.

Toni reappeared and Agatha got hurriedly to her feet. "Maybe see you later," she said to Sylvan. He rose to his feet to hold the police station door open for them.

"Don't worry," he whispered, putting an arm around Agatha's shoulders and pulling her against his body. "Soon this will all be forgotten."

"Unless these murders are solved, not by me," said Agatha, pulling away.

In the car, Agatha told Toni about Felicity being adopted. "But there's something else," she added.

"What's that? I had the most awful grilling," said Toni. "I almost felt like confessing to the murders just to get it over with."

"You know Sylvan went onto the boat."

"Yes."

"When he hugged me there, I felt the crackle of papers from his inside pocket—a lot of papers. Now, our elegant friend would not go around distorting the line of his tailored jacket with a big bunch of papers. What if he took something from the boat?"

"I couldn't see any papers lying around," said Toni.

"He might have known where to look."

"We'll go out to the house now and ask Olivia about Felicity. Then maybe we could watch somewhere on the road afterwards to see if Sylvan leaves."

"But he's already out of the house," said Toni.

"I know. But he was wearing a light suit and the weather's turning chilly. He may return to change. We wait until he leaves and then return to Olivia. You keep her talking while I say I'm going to the loo and I'll have a quick look in his room."

"How will you know which one it is? It's a big house."

"I'll follow my nose. He smells of some sort of sandal-wood scent."

"I wish we could hide somewhere in the house instead," said Toni.

"Why?"

"I would like to hear what Sylvan and Olivia have to talk about."

"Let's ask her about Felicity before we do anything else."

Olivia at first protested vehemently that Felicity was indeed her own daughter. Then she all at once broke down and sobbed out that Felicity had been adopted. George had always wanted children and it had been a great disappointment to him when she couldn't have any. Then he went off on business to Spain one time on his own. Several months later, he confessed he'd had an affair and that the woman was pregnant. Olivia threatened a divorce, but he'd pleaded with her that this was the opportunity to have the child they'd always wanted. At last she agreed. He brought the baby home. Olivia had fallen in love with the little baby. George never told her the name of the mother and she didn't want to know.

"It'll be on the adoption papers," said Agatha.

"George said he hadn't bothered about formalities, and for the last six months before the arrival of the baby, I agreed to appear pregnant."

"But how did he get the baby into the country?" asked Toni.

"He brought it by our boat."

"There are surely customs checks at the harbour?" said Agatha.

"Oh, he said, the men knew him. The baby was fast asleep in a locker and they never looked."

Agatha stared at her open-mouthed. What else had George been bringing into the country under the noses of the customs men?

"Do you happen to know if the mother was Spanish?" asked Toni.

"I suppose so."

"But she was very fair-skinned."

"Some Spaniards are. Oh, please, don't tell the police. We would be arrested and I have had so much to bear."

They waited until she had recovered. "All right," said Agatha reluctantly.

"Who told you?" demanded Olivia.

Agatha racked her brains. Someone in the village? Hardly. The police? No.

"It was Sylvan," said Olivia bitterly. "I know it must have been. He never liked me."

Agatha cleared her throat. "I'm afraid we have some bad news."

"Bad news? There can't be anything worse than murder."

"Sean Fitzpatrick has been murdered."

For one moment, Olivia looked as she were about to faint. Her bright red lipstick was the only bright colour on her white face. "Sean," she whispered at last. "Why Sean?"

"Was he a close friend of your husband?" asked Agatha.

She put out a trembling hand as if to ward off any more questions. "Enough. I can't take any more. I am going to take a sedative and go to bed. If the police call, tell them I am indisposed and will answer any questions tomorrow."

"Do you want us to help you?" asked Agatha.

"Just leave me alone!" Olivia rose and stumbled from the room.

Toni and Agatha waited in silence and then Agatha whispered, "I forgot to ask her where her husband was and when he's expected back. That boat of George's. All this security."

"I wonder if he was smuggling in anything more than just one baby," said Toni.

"Could be. It would explain a lot. But not much about Felicity's death. If we wait until Olivia settles down, I could have a look in Sylvan's room."

"But he'll still have the papers on him," Toni pointed out.

"There might be something else there. Look, Toni, why

don't you go back to the harbour and find out what you can about Sean."

"How will you get back?"

"I'll phone for a cab."

Agatha waited and waited in the silent house. At last she rose and made her way up the thickly carpeted stairs. Most of the bedroom doors stood open. Even Olivia had left her door open and Agatha could see that she was fast asleep.

She made her way along a corridor, peering into rooms until she came to a closed door at the end. She tried the handle but the door was locked.

Agatha fished out a credit card she rarely used and inserted it in the lock.

"It helps if you have a key," said an amused French voice behind her. Agatha turned round, her face flaming.

"I was just taking a look around," she said defiantly. "I am supposed to be detecting."

"The police are downstairs," said Sylvan. "Where is Olivia?"

"Taken a sedative and gone to bed."

"Then you had better go down there and tell them that."

·   ·   ·

Agatha had a few brief words with the police downstairs. Boase said he would call again in the morning. Agatha hesitated. Sylvan had not followed her down.

She felt suddenly weary and rather frightened. She longed to be back in Carsely. Agatha did not know that her wish was soon to be granted.

Chapter Five

Toni and Agatha had breakfast the next morning. Toni had found out very little about Fitzpatrick. He had "kept himself to himself," according to the locals.

Their breakfast was interrupted by the arrival of Detective Sergeant Falcon. "Mrs. Bross-Tilkington does not require your services anymore and she demands that you leave her alone. You may submit a bill for the days you have worked for her. We, the police, suggest you both return to your homes, leaving us your addresses. All you are doing is muddying a police investigation."

Agatha's protests were weaker than they might have been. Home! Back to her cottage and cats.

At last she asked, "Has Mr. Bross arrived back?"

"Yes, last night. He also wants you to leave."

"You seem almost relieved," accused Toni when the detective had left.

"Well, I am. I can't seem to concentrate here. I'd like to get back to my usual surroundings and have a good hard think. Maybe I'll just phone Olivia and make sure she doesn't want us," said Agatha, taking out her mobile.

Olivia herself answered and began to cry as soon as she heard Agatha's voice. The phone was seized from her and George's voice, truculent with rage, came on the line. "Get the hell out of here, you old bat," he roared, "or I'll make you wish you'd—"

Agatha hung up on him.

"It seems that George is the one who doesn't want us. Let's pay our bills, Toni, and get out of here."

Agatha, in her own car, followed Toni's small car as far as Mircester, shouted goodbye to her, and then drove herself home. How friendly the Cotswolds did seem after the bleakness of Downboys. It was a brisk windy day and the trees lining the steep road down to Carsely seemed to bow down in welcome as Agatha sped past.

Doris Simpson, Agatha's cleaner, was working when Agatha let herself in. She was one of the few people in Carsely who called Agatha by her first name. "You look as if you could do with a nice cup of tea," said Doris, switching off the vacuum.

"I could do with a stiff gin and tonic. I'll get it. Where are my cats?"

"They're over at my place, playing with my cat, Scrabble. I'll bring them over after I've finished here. Will you be going to the meeting in the village hall tomorrow night?"

"Too tired. What's it about anyway?"

"Thinking of ways to raise money for the pub."

"Oh, dear. I've got to go. I promised Mrs. Bloxby I'd do something to help and I forgot all about it."

"Well, just you get your drink and rest up. You really look tired."

"Is James home?"

"I saw him yesterday."

Agatha resisted an impulse to rush next door. Doris had said she looked tired. She went upstairs to the bathroom and let out a squawk of dismay. There were dark shadows under her eyes and two nasty hairs growing on her upper lip. She got rid of the hairs and then rinsed her face in cold water. After showering, she applied some skin-tightening cream before carefully making up her face and brushing her thick brown hair until it shone. She changed into a white cotton blouse and linen trousers.

Downstairs, she poured herself a stiff drink and lit a cigarette. Felicity's murder, she reflected, would be the first case she had ever given up on. Her eyes began to close and soon she was asleep. Doris came in quietly and stubbed out Agatha's cigarette in the ashtray.

Agatha was awakened two hours later by the sound of Doris returning with the cats. They did not seem particularly glad to see her, but then they never did after she had been away, punishing her in their cat way for what they saw as her neglect.

I'm getting old, thought Agatha, after she had paid Doris. I'm losing energy. Then she remembered she had barely slept the night before, trying to work out reasons for the two murders and there had been the long drive home.

Feeling better, she went upstairs again and refreshed her make-up before going to call on James. He answered the door and said abruptly, "Come in. I've just been reading about this other murder in the morning papers."

"Let me see," said Agatha eagerly.

"Sit down. I'll get you a coffee."

Agatha began to read the newspapers. There was very little hard information. There was no background on Sean at all, except that he earned money doing odd jobs— working on other people's boats and occasional carpentry and gardening jobs. No mention of grieving relatives. But the press had got hold of Felicity's previous fiancés and had also interviewed the village boys. Without actually saying so, they had pictured Felicity as some sort of nymphomaniac. Her latest fiancé, whom she had nearly married, James Lacey, was unavailable for comment. George and Olivia must be furious, thought Agatha.

When James came back with a mug of coffee for her, Agatha said, "I thought the press would be at your door."

"They were yesterday. They'll probably be back."

"Did you know Felicity was not Olivia's daughter?"

"No! How did you find that out?"

"It's odd. First Sylvan tells me Felicity was a result of an affair Olivia had and then Olivia tells me Felicity was the result of an affair George had, and before I could follow it up, the police told me Olivia wanted me to drop the case and told me to get out of town.

"I'll get into the office and ask Patrick to ferret around with his police contacts and see what he can dig up about Sean. Have the police been to see you?"

"Yes, they checked up on me yesterday to make sure I hadn't left the village."

"Are you going to the village hall tomorrow?"

"Oh, about the pub? I suppose so. If we can raise enough money, it means John Fletcher can find the money to put in an outside smoking area with heaters for the cold weather. I don't approve of smoking, but the smoking ban means the end of a lot of village pubs."

"How are you feeling?" asked Agatha.

"How do you think? Like a dirty old man."

"Come on. She wasn't a teenager."

"I could only see the beauty," said James sadly and Agatha once more felt old and frumpy.

"I'd better get to the office." She rose stiffly to her feet.

"Shouldn't you rest up a bit? You look tired."

"That's all I need," said Agatha bitterly.

On her road to the office, she was struck with an idea about how to raise interest in the pub extension. The office was empty apart from Mrs. Freedman. She said that Patrick and Phil were out on jobs. "We really need someone else," she said.

"I'll put an ad in," said Agatha. "I'll draft it out later." She picked up the phone and began to dial. She phoned every newspaper, magazine and television station she could think of, promising them that as she was still working on the Felicity case, that if they supported her in covering the meeting at the town hall, she would tip them off as soon as the case was about to break. Then she drafted out an advertisement for a detective in the local papers and gave it to Mrs. Freedman to phone in.

She hoped for publican John Fletcher's sake that the press would take the bait.

Then she left, got in her car and drove back to the Red Lion in Carsely.

"You want me to *what?*" asked John.

"I want you to break down a bit, sob, sniffle, something like that. Look. If you look sympathetic enough and it gets on local TV, you'll get donations. Come on. A sniffle or two is worth it."

"I'll feel such a fool."

"Do you want your damn pub or not?" snapped Agatha.

"Yes, but—"

"So sniffle."

Mrs. Bloxby, who had been elected to the parish council, was on the platform with the other councillors the following evening, along with John Fletcher. Agatha hissed that she and James needed chairs on the platform as well; otherwise the press would try to interview James and the pub would be forgotten.

The village hall was packed and the press had turned out in force. Mrs. Bloxby was well aware that Agatha knew how to handle this crowd better than any of them, and so the dismayed members of the parish council, who had hoped for their moment in front of the cameras, heard Mrs. Bloxby announce that Mrs. Raisin would explain why funds were needed.

Agatha knew the press wanted sound bites, so she started by hammering, "This nanny state, the worst this country has known since the days of Cromwell," and then went on to say that if the pub, that centre of social life in the village, closed down, then the village would lose its heart.

Even the antismokers in the audience were on her side because the weekly quiz game was disrupted with the smokers nipping outside for a cigarette, not to mention the darts competition and the snooker competition.

Then she called John Fletcher to the microphone with "Here is our landlord to say a few words. Poor John is nervous," said Agatha with a laugh. She produced a large handkerchief and wiped his face. The handkerchief had been soaked in onion juice from good old-fashioned garden onions. John choked and sniffled and the tears ran down his honest red face. He tried several times to speak but was overcome by the effect of the onions.

"There, there," said Agatha soothingly, leading him back to his chair and whipping her handkerchief away from him. She returned to the microphone and shouted, "Three cheers for John!" The cheers were deafening. Agatha signalled to the village band at the side, who broke into a rendering of "Jerusalem," followed by "Land of Hope and Glory."

James looked on in wry amusement. It was vulgar and at the same time magnificent. Agatha had made arrangements for Boy Scouts to go up and down the aisles collecting donations.

Agatha had moved the village hall meeting back to the earlier time of five o'clock in the hope that it would be easier to get articles in the morning papers. Her luck was in. Film of the meeting was shown on BBC's *Midlands Today* news just before seven o'clock.

. . .

Charles was entertaining a lady friend, Tessa Anderson, to pre-dinner drinks in his study because his aunt was in the drawing room with the television sound turned up high. Tessa would make a good wife, thought Charles. She was tall, which was a disadvantage as he was only of medium height. But she was a rich divorcee with extremely good looks and a large fortune. Not that he was mercenary, he tried to tell his conscience, it was just that the estate ate up money.

They were sitting side by side on a sofa. He put down his drink and decided the time had come to kiss her. Then the unmistakable voice of Agatha Raisin boomed out of the other room.

Charles shot up and ran into the drawing room. Tessa, who had closed her eyes in anticipation of that kiss, opened them again and stared about her, wondering where he had gone.

Bill Wong joined the others who were crowded around the television set in the squad room to watch Agatha's performance. Collins joined him. "Glad to see she's back to doing PR. All she was really fit for anyway. I bet the police down at Hewes are glad she's out of their hair."

But Agatha had also talked to the newspapers about the murders in Hewes, saying she regretted nothing seemed to be happening to solve the murders and promised a reward to anyone who could give her information on Sean Fitzpatrick. Agatha felt sure if she could find out about Sean, then the trail might lead back to Felicity.

Agatha felt she had now done all she could do about the Hewes affair as she drove to her office the following morning.

The next couple of days found her back in the old routine of searching for missing teenagers, cats, dogs and tracking down faithless lovers or husbands. Mrs. Freedman told her she had lined up interviews for the following day so that Agatha could hire a new detective.

"They're won't be another Toni," mourned Agatha. "What a fool I was!"

"Why?" asked Mrs. Freedman curiously.

But Agatha did not want to tell her that it was her own jealousy of Toni that had made her encourage the girl to set up her own detective agency.

She began the interviews the following day. The candidates were mostly young, barely educated, and had peculiar fantasies about what the work involved. Mrs. Freedman had gone home and Agatha was thinking about locking up when the office door opened and Toni walked in.

"Oh, it's you!" cried Agatha. "I thought for one awful minute it was one of those morons after a job here."

"This moron is looking for her job back," said Toni quietly.

"Sit down. What happened? Have you had a row with Harry?"

"Worse than that. Betty Talent, that genius who was handling the books, she's decamped and cleared out the bank account."

"Have you phoned the police?"

"Yes, I spoke to Bill."

"How on earth did she do it?"

"She seemed so ultracompetent. We left all the billing and bookkeeping to her. She had a chequebook for office supplies, petty cash, things like that."

"Was there much?"

"Harry had originally put two hundred and fifty thousand pounds of his inheritance to get us started, buying expensive equipment, paying staff, and so on. But we had at least begun to make money. There was over six thousand pounds in the account. She's not at her address. Gone, vanished." A tear ran down Toni's cheek.

"Where is Harry?"

"Said he was going back to Cambridge to see if he could

resume his studies. I was frightened to ask you, then I saw your ad."

"Of course you can have your job back, and welcome."

"I trusted Betty," wailed Toni.

"Let's go for a drink and we'll work out what to do," said Agatha. "Was it just the money? Did she pinch anything else out of the office?"

"A couple of cameras and a telephoto lens."

"Bitch. Let's go."

In a corner of The George pub, Agatha, after she had fetched drinks from the bar, pulled out a notebook and pen from her capacious handbag. "Let me see," she began. "Was the office rented?"

"Yes. Rent paid. Oh, I should have guessed something. The estate agency phoned up two months ago and said the rent was in arrears. Betty turned very red but said she would go round and pay them immediately. I should have suspected something even then."

"Now, office equipment, computers and stuff?"

"Still there."

"We'll sell that and you continue with outstanding cases and collect the money for any you solve."

Charles came and joined them. "Saw your car outside," he said cheerfully.

"Buy your own drink," said Agatha huffily. She had not forgiven him for running away from Hewes.

Charles shortly returned carrying a half of lager. "What's going on?" he asked. "Toni, you look as if you've been crying."

In a sad little voice, Toni described what had happened.

When she had finished, Agatha surveyed Charles's well-tailored figure. "You've stayed with me a lot, haven't you, Charles?"

"Yes, dear."

"You have eaten my food, haven't you?"

"If you can call microwaved curries food, yes."

"So you owe me." Agatha's bearlike eyes bored into his face.

"My dear, Aggie, if you want to have sex with me, you only have to ask."

"Don't be flippant. I've got a lot of work and so has Toni. I've got this pub business to follow through."

"Saw you on the box. Real tub-thumping perfor—"

"I want you to find Betty Talent."

"But Toni's got the police on to it."

"They won't do much. Oh, have you a photo?"

Toni had a folder and produced one. "I gave the rest to Bill."

Betty Talent was undoubtedly a plain-looking girl with a sallow face and dark brown hair pulled back in a knot.

"I'll do my best," said Charles. "Give me her address. I'll start there."

But instead of going straight to Betty Talent's address, Charles waited until the following morning and went to see James Lacey.

After James had welcomed him, Charles explained that Agatha had bulldozed him into finding the missing Betty Talent, after telling James how Betty had absconded with the money.

"You could always have said no," James pointed out.

"To Agatha? You must be joking. Anyway, that's why I'm here."

"I can't see—"

"You can pick locks, can't you?"

"Yes, but—"

"Then get your jacket. We're off to break into Betty's flat."

The flat was over a grocer's shop in Berry's Wynd, one of the narrow medieval streets behind the abbey.

"If the street door is locked, I can't stand in broad daylight picking the lock," complained James.

"We won't know until we try it," said Charles. "Come on."

They crossed the street. Charles turned the handle of the street door. It swung open.

"See," he said. "Faint heart never won successful burglary."

"What if there's more than two flats?" whispered James.

"It's just a little Pakistani grocer's," muttered Charles impatiently as they mounted the stairs. "See! One flat. I'll knock first."

He knocked very loudly. "There's a bell," said James.

Charles leaned on it. No reply.

"Okay," said Charles. "Get to work."

James pulled out a set of skeleton keys. "I remembered you had a set of those," said Charles. "Where did you get them?"

"I took them off someone a long time ago."

"Does it always take this long?" complained Charles after ten minutes.

"Shut up. This isn't a movie and there are two locks here. We really should have checked in the grocery store first. No doubt they own this flat. Maybe they've already re-rented it. Ah, here we go." The door opened.

They found themselves inside a small two-roomed flat with a tiny bathroom and a minuscule kitchen behind a curtain. Charles started searching in the bedroom while James searched the living room.

"Her clothes are still in the wardrobe," said Charles. "Very dowdy they are, too."

"There's hair dye in the bathroom," called James. "She's gone blonde by the look of it."

Charles wandered back in. "She's left nothing else apart from the clothes. No sign of any personal papers or passport."

"And no toothbrush in the bathroom," said James.

Charles peered out of the kitchen window and down into the area at the back.

"Thank God for the new lousy rubbish collections. There are bins down there. Feel like some bin diving? We may find some clue as to where she's gone."

"How do we get to the area?" asked James.

"I saw a lane at the side of the shop."

"What if someone comes out of the back of the shop and asks us what we are doing?"

"They won't because we are going to go into the shop and tell them why we want to search the rubbish and ask them to tell us which is Betty's."

A large woman in a sari behind the counter raised her hands in horror when they explained about Betty being a thief. She summoned a small boy and told him to show them the bin where Miss Talent put her rubbish.

"Now," said Charles, " all this recycling is great because we don't want the small green food bin, we want that big grey one."

James opened the lid. "Not much. We'd better tip it over and go through the stuff."

"Carrier bags," said James triumphantly. "Look at this. Victoria's Secret, Ghost and Armani."

"And look what I've found," said Charles, holding up a brochure. "A cruise on the *Southern Cross*. Sails to the Caribbean. Wait a bit. Sails tomorrow morning. Passengers on board this evening. I bet she's there, all blonded up and dressed up in poor Harry's money. Let's go."

"Wouldn't it be easier just to tell the police and have her arrested?" asked James.

"Where's the thrill of the hunt? Let's find her first and then call the police. Come on. It'll be worth it for Aggie."

Betty Talent unpacked her new clothes and hung them away in her first-class cabin. She ran her hands down the fine material of the clothes and grinned as she thought about the shock Toni would get when she was told all their money had gone. She detested Toni. Toni had always been one of the prettiest and most popular girls in the school.

She studied her new appearance in the mirror and patted her blonde hair. Gone was shivering, frightened Betty Talent. She felt reborn. There came a knock at the cabin door. She smiled. Probably that good-looking purser back again to see if she was all right.

Betty swung open the cabin door, a welcoming smile

on her face which slowly faded. The captain stood there. Behind him stood two police officers, and behind the police officers, two men, one of whom she recognized as Charles Fraith. When Toni had thrown an opening party at the agency, Charles had escorted Agatha to it. She also recognized James Lacey because James had invited Toni and the other members of the agency to his engagement party, although Betty had not been invited to the wedding. If only I had stolen someone's passport, Betty thought wildly.

As the captain confirmed her name, a policeman charged her with theft. All her sunny dreams came crashing down about her ears.

It was left to Charles to phone Agatha with the good news. She asked to speak to James, but when Charles held his mobile out, James muttered, "Talk to her later."

"What's up with you?" asked Charles. "You might have had a word with her."

"I don't know," said James. "I just wish they'd find the murderer. I've an awful feeling the police suspect me. I was going to go away on my travels again but when I called in at Mircester police headquarters, they called Hewes police, who said I was not to leave the country until they contacted me and gave me permission."

Charles thought briefly of Tessa. Should he pursue his

courtship? But the fact that he had doubts about it made him hesitant. "Look, you and I could go to Hewes and do a bit of detecting, couldn't we? Better than sitting on our bums and waiting forever."

"I don't see what we can find out that the police cannot," said James.

"Oh, really? Well, we just found Betty. If they'd gone through her rubbish, they'd have found the same clue. And another thing—I don't think the police had even been around to her flat or the Pakistanis wouldn't have been so surprised. They've got so many government targets to meet, they might drop this case and go on to arresting something easier, like a speeding motorist."

Bill Wong joined Agatha and Toni that evening shortly after they had received the good news. They had left a message for him that they were having dinner in The George, the pub across the square from police headquarters. But they had finished their meal by the time Bill arrived.

"That was good work finding Betty," he said. "Sorry, I couldn't get away earlier. Of course everyone is blaming everyone else for not having checked the girl's garbage. Detective Sergeant Collins was supposed to be on it, but she hates you both so, she probably did the minimum. The latest is that the captain is going to refund the money Betty paid for her cruise, and just over one hundred and fifty thousand pounds was found in her luggage, along with the missing cameras." He smiled at Toni. "So it looks as if you can get your detective agency back again."

"'Fraid not," said Toni. "I phoned Harry as soon as I got the news but he says he's decided to go back to university even if the money is recovered. I don't want to run it on my own. I'm only sorry that my friend, Sharon Gold, is out of a job."

"Is that the one who changes hair colour every week, and has a pierced navel always on display?"

"That's the one," said Toni.

"Oh, she'll do," said Agatha, feeling magnanimous. "I need someone who can go round the clubs and pubs and not look like a detective." Agatha was delighted to have Toni back again.

While Toni phoned Sharon with the good news, Agatha asked Bill, "Anything from Hewes?"

"They wouldn't tell me anything."

"I'll phone Patrick. Maybe he's dug up something."

Agatha phoned Patrick and listened hard. When she had rung off, she said, "Sean Fitzpatrick's real name was Jimmy Donnell, once IRA, but became an informer for British Intelligence for a couple of years. So the Hewes police think his murder was nothing to do with Felicity's."

Agatha scowled horribly. "It all doesn't add up. Boats! Felicity was smuggled into Britain as a baby. I wonder if they've charged George Bross with that?"

"I doubt it," said Bill. "George is a Freemason and a generous contributor to police charities."

"But think! All that security around the house! Maybe they were smuggling something like drugs or arms in."

She phoned Patrick again. They all fell silent until Agatha had finished her call.

"Evidently both Sean or whatever his name was and George both had their boats practically taken apart. Nothing there. And that Jerry dog minder hasn't even got a criminal record."

"Someone told me that you've been saying to the press that you are offering a reward."

"I thought that might stir something up."

"Agatha," said Bill sternly, "I should think you've enough work on your hands at the moment. I assume you've got Toni's cases to clear up as well as your own. Just let the police get on with their job."

"Hah, bloody hah."

"I'm serious. Leave it alone."

Agatha did find that all her energy in the following six weeks had to be poured into the work of the agency. Sharon proved bright and willing, although Agatha felt she would never get used to the girl's appearance. Although chubby, Sharon favoured very tight jeans and boob tubes. Her masses of hair had recently been dyed black with blonde streaks.

There was no James next door. He had received permission to go off on his travels. With James out of the picture, Charles was no longer interested in detecting anything, finally feeling, in his lazy way, he had done his bit finding Betty.

Agatha found she was not looking forward to a lonely weekend. Toni was going with Sharon to a rock concert. She did not want to impose her company on Mrs. Bloxby, knowing that lady was overburdened with parish affairs. Even though she was sure of a great welcome at the pub, where the new smoking section had been set up outside, thanks to generous donations and to the free services offered by local builders and carpenters, she did not want to go on her own.

So she received with pleasure a phone call from Roy Silver, asking to visit for the weekend.

Roy was delighted with his welcome but surprised that nothing had been happening about Felicity's murder. "You know," he said, "this may be the very first time you've been unsuccessful."

"I don't like the sound of that," said Agatha. "If it were anywhere in the Cotswolds I might have better luck, but if I go back to Downboys, the Hewes police will resent the very sight of me."

The phone rang. Agatha went to answer it. She hoped it might be Sylvan. She had forgotten he was a philanderer and at the back of her mind there was always the hope that he might ring her up.

But it was Bert Trymp on the phone. "Remember me?" he asked.

"Yes, of course. You work at the garage in Downboys."

"There was something in the papers about a reward."

"Yes, there was," said Agatha cautiously.

"How much?"

"If the news is worth it, five thousand."

There was a silence. Then Bert said, "You'd best meet me down here. On my boat. I live on it. It's called the *Southern Flyer*. It's an old fishing boat in the harbour at Hewes."

"Let me see," said Agatha. "Tomorrow's Saturday. I could get down there around lunchtime. How can I find your boat?"

"You know the one where that fellow was murdered?"

"Could never forget it."

"I'm five boats along to the right o' that. It's an old fishing boat," he repeated.

"I'll be there," said Agatha.

She told Roy. "I'm not going to bother Patrick or Phil," she said. "There might be nothing in it. But the weather's lovely. Like to come?"

Roy looked anxious. "I haven't anything nautical to wear."

"Don't even think about it. Any clothes will do."

Chapter Six

THEY LEFT THE Cotswolds in blazing sunshine with shafts of golden light shining through the green tunnels of trees covering the road out of Carsely.

But as they drove steadily on, a bank of grey cloud rose up on the horizon and soon rain began to smear the windscreen. "I'm not really dressed for this," complained Roy, who had dug a striped French fisherman's sweater out of his capacious luggage.

"We brought our coats. They're in the boot with the rest of the luggage," said Agatha reassuringly. "We won't freeze."

To Agatha's relief, the skies began to clear as they drove

down to the harbour at Hewes. "It's a river!" exclaimed Roy. "I thought we were going to the sea."

"It leads down to the sea," said Agatha. "Let's get out and look for Bert's boat. It's an old fishing boat."

"Don't ask me," said Roy, getting a coat out of the car boot. "I never could tell one boat from another except the ones with sails are yachts. Anyway, he's probably dead."

"What on earth makes you think that?"

"Well, it's like in books and movies. Someone says, 'The name of the murderer is . . . aargh.' They always get bumped off."

"I don't believe it. We'll find him." How irritating not to be in the police but always poking around on the outside of any investigation.

"I think that must be it," she said. "It's the shabbiest of the lot and it does look like a small fishing boat. Yes, I can make out the name. It's the *Southern Flyer*."

The deck and wheelhouse were deserted. "We'd best go aboard," said Agatha.

They climbed onto the deck, shouting loudly, "Bert! Bert!" while the mocking seagulls sailed about overhead.

"The wind's whipping our voices away," said Agatha. "Let's try below."

"Must we?" pleaded Roy. "I'm feeling seasick already."

"Then stay where you are. I'll go down."

But Agatha found the door to the cabin firmly locked. She retreated back up on deck. "No one there. I just said we'd meet around lunchtime. It's just noon. Let's go back to the car and wait. He'll have to pass us to get to his boat."

They waited and waited while the rising wind rocked the car and the sky grew dark overhead. Suddenly the rain poured down in floods. Agatha switched on the windscreen wipers and continued to watch. At last, the shower passed and the sun shone out again.

"You wait here," said Agatha. "I'll try the harbour office."

But that office was closed. Agatha wandered up and down the row of moored boats until she saw a man working on his deck.

She called out, "Have you seen Bert Trymp?"

"That's his boat along there, the *Southern Flyer*," he called back.

"He's not on it."

"Then try his father's garage in Downboys. Do you need directions?"

"I know the way," said Agatha.

"I'm hungry," complained Roy when Agatha got back into the car.

"So am I," said Agatha. "Look, there's a café over there. We can get some sandwiches and coffee and then get off to Downboys."

•　　•　　•

"What happened to nice vulgar white-bread sandwiches?" mourned Roy after lunch as Agatha drove them to Down-boys. "It's always that nasty brown bread which tastes of bitter malt. *And* mayonnaise on everything. *And* all wrapped in plastic. No one makes a real sandwich anymore. And that ham! It was so slippery and shiny, I could see my face in it."

"I'll get you a good dinner this evening. Here is Down-boys and here is the garage and . . . would you believe it? It's closed for Saturday. Isn't that so bloody British? No wonder half our businesses are being outsourced abroad."

"Calm down, sweetie," said Roy. "There's a house next to it. Bet that's where they live."

Agatha marched up to the bungalow next to the garage and rang the bell.

"I say, Aggie," said Roy, grabbing her arm. "I've just seen a fawn."

"There might be deer round here."

"No, a man who looks like—"

He broke off as the door opened. A short thickset man stood there. He had a pugnacious face, small grey eyes and a thatch of unkempt grey hair.

"Mr. Trymp?" ventured Agatha.

"Who's asking?"

"My name is Agatha Raisin and this is Roy Silver. Your son wanted to see us on his boat at lunchtime today but we can't find him."

"I don't know where he is. He lives on that stupid wreck down in the harbour. Try there."

"We have but he's not on board."

"Can't help."

"Mr. Trymp, may we come in?"

"No."

"I am a private detective. I have offered a reward for any information about the death of the man who called himself Sean Fitzpatrick."

"I 'member you. You're that bird what was married to the fellow who was going to marry Felicity. I think our Bert's been playing games. He don't know nothing."

"How can you know that?"

"'Cos I know my son and he's as thick as pig shit!" Mr. Trymp slammed the door in their faces.

"Now what?" asked Agatha gloomily. "Why are you staring about like that?"

"I saw this chap watching us. He looked like a fawn. No, well, maybe like one of those Pan creatures in the old paintings."

"Did he have grey hair, hooded eyes, slim figure?"

"That's him."

"That, if I am not mistaken, was Sylvan Dubois. You must have seen him at the wedding. Not like you to fail to notice someone like him. Why on earth did he not come over and speak to us? You know, Roy, much as I hate to do it, I'd better go to the police and tell them about Bert's phone call. He may be lying dead in his boat."

After a long wait at the police station, they were ushered in to face Detective Sergeant Falcon.

He listened carefully while Agatha told him about Bert's phone call. When she had finished, he said, "You can now leave matters with us, Mrs. Raisin."

"Oh, no, you don't!" said Agatha. "You'd never have heard about it if it hadn't been for me. I'm coming with you."

Back to the harbour under a squally sky. Boats and yachts were bobbing at anchor. "You two wait here," commanded Falcon. He and a policeman went on board. Falcon eventually emerged. "I'll get the boy's father down here and tell him to bring any keys."

The man from the harbour office came strolling along. "What's up?"

"We think something may have happened to Bert Trymp, Mr. Judson," said Falcon. "Did he leave keys with you?"

"Yes, as a matter of fact. They're on a nail in the office."

"Where anyone might have got hold of them while that lazy sod is in the pub," muttered Falcon.

They waited impatiently. Judson came back with a ring

of keys. Falcon took them, and accompanied again by the policeman, went back on board. Agatha pulled her coat more tightly around her.

"Here comes Sylvan," said Roy.

Agatha looked along the quay and saw Sylvan strolling towards them. He came up to Agatha and kissed her on both cheeks and then asked cheerfully, "Any more bodies?"

"Do you know where Bert is?" asked Agatha.

He shrugged and spread his hands.

"We were up at the garage," pursued Agatha. "Why didn't you speak to us?"

"Things to do," he said lazily. "Places to go. Why are you looking for Bert? I assume that is why the police are here."

"He said he had information about Sean's murder."

"But it has been established that Sean or whatever he was really called was killed by the IRA."

"And where's the proof of that?" demanded Agatha angrily. She was angry because those kisses had given her a flutter.

"I don't know," said Sylvan, "but the police seem sure of it." He raised his expressive eyebrows in the direction of Roy.

"This is a friend of mine, Roy Silver. Roy, Sylvan Dubois."

"Charmed," tittered Roy.

"Why don't you both join me for dinner tonight?" asked Sylvan.

"We didn't really mean to stay . . ." began Agatha, but Roy chipped in with "That would be lovely. I mean, Aggie, we can hardly leave without finding out what happened to Bert."

"All right," said Agatha. "Where?"

"There's a very good Cantonese restaurant called China Dreams on the main street," said Sylvan. "Shall we say eight o'clock?"

He turned to leave. "Aren't you going to wait and see if the police find anything?" asked Agatha.

"If they had, they'd be leaping about by now. À bientôt!"

Falcon eventually reappeared. "No sign of him," he called to Agatha. "He probably was playing a trick on you. But we'll keep looking."

"Now what?" asked Roy.

"I want to find a Marks and Spencer," said Agatha, "and buy some clean underwear and a nightie. We may as well stay the night."

After they had booked rooms in The Jolly Farmer and done their shopping, Agatha said, "We've still got time until this evening. I'd like to have a look at the bottom of the Brosses' property. Bert might be working on a boat there."

"We could go back to the harbour and see if anyone will take us down the river," suggested Roy.

"Good idea."

But Judson said he didn't know of anyone available. They did not say where they wanted to go, only that they wanted to sail down the river for a bit. "I've a dinghy you can rent," said Judson, "but I don't think you'd know how to handle one of those."

Roy looked out over the water. The sun was shining and the wind had dropped. He had only ever had one lesson, but he knew Agatha often thought he was a wimp and wanted to impress her. "I can handle a dinghy," he said eagerly.

"Are you sure?" asked Agatha nervously.

"Oh, sure as sure."

Agatha was impressed when Roy got the sail up and the dinghy began to move swiftly down the river. Roy was proud of himself as he tacked backwards and forwards down the river.

Then the wind returned with a roar and Agatha screamed as the dinghy heeled dangerously.

"Do something!" shouted Agatha. "My bum's wet."

Roy scrambled to lower the sail but the boat was now caught in a strong current and they were borne at what seemed like a terrifying rate. Just when they both feared they would be taken right down the river and out to sea, the current drove the dinghy straight into a group of willows on a headland just after the Brosses' property. They seized the branches and held on.

Roy swung onto the shore by the branches and grabbed the dinghy's tender and made the boat fast. He helped a shaken Agatha ashore. They both sat down on the muddy, grassy bank. Agatha's face was white. "You silly chump," she said. "You told me you knew how to handle the thing."

Roy shivered. "You know, that Judson must have known it was dangerous. He must know all about that current. I'll pull the dinghy up on the bank and he can collect it. If those willow branches hadn't been blown down so near the water, we'd have had it. Let's get back to the pub. I'm freezing."

Agatha was recovering. She took out her mobile phone and asked directory enquiries for Judson's number and then dialled him. She blasted him for having risked their lives. He shouted back that they were incompetent until Agatha threatened to go to the police. He said he would come down the river, collect the dinghy and take them back. Roy, with a sinking heart, heard Agatha say, "We'll find our own way back."

"Why?" asked Roy miserably.

"Because, as we scooted past, I saw the Bross house through the trees. If we walk back along the riverbank, we'll be able to get to Bross's boat. Bert might be there. If he's not, we'll find a way round the property to the village and phone for a taxi."

They squelched their way along under a now lowering sky. They rounded a bend and came to the stretch of river in front of the house but there was no boat at anchor. "Snakes and bastards!" complained Agatha. There was a short wooden jetty. She walked to the edge and stared up and down the river.

"Oh, come on. Let's get out of here," pleaded Roy.

Agatha was about to turn away when the movement of something in the water below the jetty caught her eye. She stared down. Under the restless movement of the river something white could be seen.

"Roy," said Agatha in a shaky voice. "I think there's something down there."

Roy trotted up and knelt down on the jetty. The water swirled and eddied and then amongst the swirls there was a sudden calm. "It's a face," he said. "Aggie, there's a body down there."

Agatha took out her phone and called the police.

Oh, how long the day seemed as darkness fell and the body of Bert Trymp was lifted from the river. Halogen lamps were set up. Teams of scene of crime operatives moved in the light in their white suits like ghosts. After the body was pulled from the water, Agatha said she thought the body was that of Bert. It was difficult because she had only met him once and the face was swollen from immersion in the river. Someone had struck him a savage blow on the back of the head, filled his pockets with rocks and dropped him off the jetty. Bert's father was collected and brought to the scene. In a gruff voice, he identified his son and then burst into tears. The Bross-Tilkingtons were abroad, said Falcon. They were on holiday in Barcelona.

Then Agatha and Roy were driven to the police station and the questioning began. Boase and Falcon seemed to find Agatha's knack of finding bodies very suspicious.

It was eleven o'clock in the evening when they were finally released. "I'm hungry," wailed Roy.

"The Chinese restaurant is still open," said a familiar voice behind them.

"What are you doing here, Sylvan?" demanded Agatha.

"I am the prime suspect. I am house-sitting for George. The body was found under his jetty. They have taken away my passport. Let's eat."

"I should really change," said Agatha. She had not only bought underwear but a sweater and trousers from Marks.

"Don't," wailed Roy. "I'm simply too hungry."

"The restaurant is only just along the street," said Sylvan.

. . .

The staff at the restaurant seemed to know Sylvan very well. They rushed to welcome him. "Shall I order for us?" asked Sylvan.

I always seem to land up with men who won't let me choose my own food, thought Agatha, but she was too tired to protest. "Go ahead."

Sylvan seemed to know a great deal of light yet scurrilous gossip about various celebrities. He poured generous amounts of wine. Agatha began to relax. She felt it would do no harm to get mildly drunk and maybe, therefore, get a good night's sleep without being plagued by nightmares of Bert's dead face.

But charming and attractive as Sylvan was, Agatha, mindful of her detective duties, finally asked, "Who do you think killed Bert?"

"I haven't a clue."

"I forgot to ask. When exactly did George and Olivia leave?"

"Yesterday, I think."

"So George could have murdered Bert!"

"Hardly. If Bert's information was about Sean, then it stands to reason that some Irishman decided to get rid of him in the same way. Sean could have had information about some IRA cell working on the mainland."

135

"But I thought the Provisional IRA had gone all peaceful," protested Roy.

"Oh, yeah?" said Agatha cynically. "Tell that to the people of Omagh."

Sylvan looked at Agatha's tired face and said sympathetically, "Why don't you go and have a good night's sleep? When do the police want to see you in the morning? I have to be there at nine o'clock."

"Same time for us," said Roy gloomily.

"Well, then, we will all meet up at the police station."

As they were making their way out of the restaurant, Agatha stopped in the doorway and said, "We didn't pay the bill!"

"I run an account here when I am in town. Don't worry about it. I invited you, remember?"

"Well, thanks awfully," gushed Roy.

Sylvan walked with them to The Jolly Farmer and at the entrance drew Agatha to him, and holding her close, kissed her tenderly on both cheeks.

"See you tomorrow."

Agatha walked up to her room in a daze. Could he really fancy her?

But after she had said goodnight to Roy, gone into her room and looked in the bathroom mirror, she let out a squawk of horror. There were deep shadows under her eyes and her hair was a tangled mess. The rain earlier had washed all her make-up off.

If only she could turn the clock back, say, twenty years, thought Agatha. She showered, put on her nightdress and plunged down into an exhausted sleep.

She was awakened at seven in the morning by Roy hammering on the door and saying they'd better get some breakfast because the police might keep them all day.

Agatha spent so much time brushing her hair and making up her face that she had only time to eat a couple of pieces of toast and gulp down a cup of coffee before it was time to go back to the police station.

This time, Agatha was interviewed by Detective Superintendent Walker, a tall stout man with a red round face like a farmer.

He was flanked by Boase and Falcon. The tape hissed quietly as Agatha was taken through her story several times. At last she was told to sign her statement and that she was free to go. Roy was already waiting for her in the reception area.

"Have you seen Sylvan?" asked Agatha.

"I asked the desk sergeant. He left just before I was released."

"I'd better phone him and see if he wants to see us." Agatha took out her mobile phone. She dialled the Brosses' home at Downboys but only got the answering service.

"You're keen on him," said Roy with a grin. "Can't say I blame you."

"I am not," protested Agatha. "He was so amusing last night that I never really got down to questioning him properly."

"We'd better pack it in. I've got to get to work tomorrow," said Roy.

Agatha paid the bill at the inn and then reluctantly drove out of Hewes. She stopped suddenly outside the town.

"What is it?" asked Roy.

"You know who was missing last night? That dog man, Jerry."

"So, he must have gone off with his boss."

"Who's looking after the dogs?"

"Sylvan, I suppose. Aggie, may I remind you I've got to get back to Carsely, pick up my stuff and catch the London train at Moreton-in-Marsh?"

Agatha sighed and drove on. Poor Bert, she thought. I've just got to find out what happened.

During the following weeks, the threat of a recession made Agatha concentrate on her work. Shares were sliding, prices were rising, petrol was a disgraceful cost and she knew that soon people would begin to think twice about the luxury of hiring a private detective. Certainly, there would always be the desperate people and the lawyers who wanted evidence for divorce cases, but all the bread-and-butter cases like missing cats, dogs, and teenagers, the backbone of the agency, would soon begin to dwindle. Old memories of poverty drove her on. She was a very rich woman and was determined to stay that way.

Toni was no longer prepared to work overtime, even for pay. For Toni was in love.

She had worked on a divorce case for a Mircester businessman, Perry Stanton. He owned a computer company out on the Mircester industrial estate. He had been so grateful to Toni for having secured the necessary evidence that his wife was having an affair that he had begun to ask her out while his divorce was going through. He was tall and handsome and in his late thirties. Toni had kept the budding relationship secret from Agatha, knowing that lady would not approve of the age difference.

She had, however, confided in Sharon Gold, who had admitted that Perry was "dreamy." Toni did not know that it all worried Sharon. Sharon knew that Toni was still a virgin and wanted the best for her friend.

Her worries heightened when Toni told her that she was taking a two-week holiday and going to Paris with Perry.

At last, Sharon could not bear it any longer and called on Agatha one Saturday at her cottage in Carsely.

Agatha reflected that she could never really get used to Sharon's appearance. Sharon had masses of hair, now dyed a flaming red. Her generous figure bulged out of a pair of brief shorts and a boob tube. Her plump legs ended in high-heeled stilettos. But Sharon had proved to be quick and clever and good on cases where she could pass unnoticed amongst crowds of young people.

Agatha listened to her carefully. She asked her if Sharon knew which Parisian hotel Toni was being taken to. Sharon took out a tiny notebook from her pink plastic handbag and flipped it open. "It's . . . here, you read it."

It was the Hotel de Notre Dame in the Rue Maître Albert on the Left Bank. Agatha frowned. "Doesn't sound very grand. I thought he would have taken her to the George V or somewhere like that. Leave it with me," said Agatha. "I'll think of something."

When Sharon had left, Agatha found Sylvan's card. Perhaps he might be in Paris. She dialled and heard that now familiar voice on the other end of the line.

She explained the situation to Sylvan and asked, "Do you know this hotel?"

"It is actually a modestly priced but very good hotel indeed. But if he has the money and is not taking her somewhere superb, then he has done it before. He may have a petite amie on the side."

"A what?"

"A mistress."

"Can you do anything?" asked Agatha.

"But certainly. Your little lady will be returned to you intact."

"Have you heard anything about Bert's murder?"

"Must go."

Toni was having second thoughts. As they got into a taxi at Charles de Gaulle Airport in Paris, the day was sunny. Suddenly Perry looked much older. But she convinced herself she was suffering from virginal nerves. Why on earth should she feel nervous when her friends leaped in and out of bed without a care in the world?

But her spirits rose as the taxi moved along the quays and she saw Notre Dame rearing up over the Seine. The hotel came as something of a shock to Toni. She knew Perry was very rich and had assumed it would be a grand hotel. Certainly the Hotel de Notre Dame at a bend in the street looked very French and very pretty.

The motherly-looking woman at the desk checked the registrations and raised her eyebrows. "But you cancelled the reservation, Mr. Stanton," she exclaimed.

"No, I did not," said Perry hotly. "Oh, well, give us another room."

"I don't have one. That room was taken almost immediately after the cancellation."

"Look, you incompetent fool—"

"Monsieur," said the woman in perfect English, "I assure you I am neither a fool nor incompetent. In any case, the room would not have been suitable. It had a double bed, and you surely do not want to sleep with your daughter."

"Let's get out of here," snarled Perry. Toni began to feel miserable. She had never really worried that much before about the age difference. "I know a place up in Saint-Germain-des-Prés," said Perry. He strode angrily ahead, pulling his small suitcase behind him. Toni hitched her satchel over her shoulder and followed him.

They had just reached Place Maubert when a tall woman with a child barred their way. "So here you are," she said. "You might have phoned me."

Perry tried to push past her. "I've never seen you before in my life," he shouted.

A crowd was beginning to gather. "Don't you know your own child?" shouted the woman. She was tall and blonde and the child, a little girl, was a charming little moppet with a head of golden curls.

The little girl held up her arms. "Papa," she said.

The row went on, Perry shouting he did not know her and the woman claiming that he had deserted her and left his daughter fatherless. She repeated it all in French for the benefit of the listening crowd.

Perry turned round desperately. "Look, Toni . . ." he began, but Toni had disappeared.

Perry swung back to the woman, beside himself with rage, and shouted, "You lying slut," and the woman translated the insult for the listeners. A market worker stepped forward and socked Perry hard on the jaw and Perry stumbled backwards and fell down on his bottom on the street.

When he struggled to his feet, the woman and child were getting into a taxi and speeding off.

He ran along the street, searching for Toni, but he could not see her anywhere.

Toni was sitting in the cool darkness of Notre Dame amongst the flickering candles. At last she went outside and walked down to the river and sat down on a bench and phoned Agatha, who pretended she was hearing about Perry for the first time.

Agatha felt that Sylvan had really gone in for overkill but when Toni had finished, she said soothingly, "Best to find out now rather than later. Are you going to the airport? Or do you want to stay on in Paris?"

"I just want to get home. Not the airport. He may be waiting there."

"Then go to Gare du Nord and get yourself a ticket on *Eurostar*. Get a return. It's cheaper, and choose a date to go back when you might want a holiday."

"I don't think I'll ever want to see Paris again," said Toni. "I'll see you soon."

· · ·

Agatha phoned Sylvan and thanked him. "You owe me, Agatha Raisin. One actress and one child actress."

"Send me a bill."

"Wouldn't dream of it. Have dinner with me."

"All right. Where?"

"I have never been to the Cotswolds. What about tomorrow night? Give me directions."

Agatha did, her heart beating hard. A little voice of caution was telling her she knew nothing about Sylvan except that when there was a murder, he was always there.

But what hurt could one dinner do her?

Chapter Seven

AGATHA CALLED ON Mrs. Bloxby the following morning. The vicar's wife had heard about the death of Bert on television. "I really don't see what the police are up to," complained the vicar's wife. "You cannot have three murders around the Bross-Tilkingtons without them being involved in some way, not to mention their French friend."

"What about the French friend?" asked Agatha defensively.

"He's always on the scene. Have you thought of that? He is house-sitting for the Bross-Tilkingtons and then a body is found under a jetty on the property right after the boy said he had information for you."

"Bert might just have fallen in and smashed his head on something," said Agatha.

"The police are treating it as murder. For your own safety, Mrs. Raisin, I would keep well clear of any of them."

Agatha realized with a sinking heart that when Sylvan called at her cottage that evening, the faces behind the twitching lace curtains of Carsely would register his presence in the village.

"As a matter of fact," said Agatha in what she hoped was a casual way, "he's taking me out for dinner tonight."

"Is that wise?"

"He's an attractive Frenchman, I'm sure he's not involved, and I haven't had any fun in ages."

"Do you mean sex?"

"You shock me."

"Just a thought. Please don't let your hormones cloud your usually sharp mind, Mrs. Raisin."

"I do owe him a favour." Agatha told Mrs. Bloxby about Toni's adventure.

"I would make sure that dinner is all he gets," said Mrs. Bloxby with unusual severity. "It may be a chance, however, to extract some more information from him. Where do you plan to take him for dinner?"

Agatha had really planned to serve a candlelit dinner at home but she said airily, "I'll think of somewhere."

But Mrs. Bloxby's remarks had caused her to think it might be better to take him out to a restaurant. And she was sure a Frenchman would not appreciate microwaveable cuisine. She booked a table at the hotel in Mircester and then did little work that day, fitting it in between visits to Evesham to go to the beautician's and then round to the hairdresser's, Achille. Her favourite hairdresser, Jeanelle, was on holiday, so the manager, Gareth, took over, pointing out that her roots were showing. Tinting meant more time that Agatha felt she had to spare, but it just had to be done.

She eventually arrived home in a panic and tore everything out of her wardrobe looking for the perfect outfit. At last dressed in a slinky black velvet gown and high heels, and with a cashmere stole over her arm, she descended to await Sylvan's arrival.

The day had been exhausting and she fell asleep, only to be awakened later by the ringing of the doorbell. She started up. The cats had been sleeping on her lap and her gown was covered in cat hairs.

Seizing a clothes brush, she hurriedly brushed down her dress and then opened the door. Sylvan stood there smiling broadly, and holding a large bouquet of red roses.

"How beautiful!" exclaimed Agatha. "Go into the sitting room and fix yourself a drink and I'll put these in water."

She seized the clothes brush from where she had left it on the hall table and attacked her dress again in the kitchen after running water in the sink and placing the bouquet in it.

She returned to join Sylvan. "I took a drive around the Cotswolds," he said. "Very beautiful."

"They say it hasn't changed in three hundred years," said Agatha, "but I think that's too romantic a view. They didn't have supermarkets and all-night shopping three hundred years ago. Mind you, on a quiet day the villages look much as they must have done long ago. That golden Cotswold limestone stands up to the weather very well. The shops are feeling the pinch. Very few Americans, what with the weak dollar."

Sylvan finished his glass of whisky. "Shall we go? I am very hungry. Or are we eating here?"

"No, I've booked us a table in Mircester."

Sylvan said he would drive. Agatha eased herself into the passenger seat of his Jaguar sports car, suppressing a moan of pain as her arthritic hip protested violently.

James Lacey had just returned home. He watched, startled, as they drove off, swore under his breath and decided to find out from Mrs. Bloxby just what Agatha was about dating a murder suspect.

. . .

"What puzzles me," said Agatha, mindful of her detective duties, "is why you told me that the baby was Olivia's and yet Olivia told me the baby was George's and he had smuggled it in. Surely the police would have found that out and charged him."

"Felicity was Olivia's daughter. Olivia has the birth certificate. There was no need to smuggle any baby in. She is a very respectable matron and thinks a man having an illegitimate baby is better than a woman having one. Very English."

"Could George have been smuggling something else? Drugs, say, or cigarettes?"

"George is just what you see—bluff and honest and very respectable."

"Your friendship with them surprises me. When we had dinner in Hewes, you talked about all sorts of glamorous people and celebrities. What is the attraction of the Bross-Tilkingtons?"

"I was very ill just after I met them. My fair-weather friends were apt to stay away, but George and Olivia stuck by me until the treatment was over. We became very close."

"This whole business at Downboys must have shocked you all badly. You know the area. What's going on? Why did they hire an ex-IRA man like Sean?"

Sylvan sighed and raised his shoulders and spread his

hands. "My dear Agatha, as far as they were concerned, he was a local yachtsman and an odd-job man. Nothing sinister there."

"But there must be something sinister," protested Agatha. "Who killed Felicity?"

He leaned across the table and took one of her hands in a warm clasp. "Are you surprised, considering the way Felicity went on? Probably some rejected lover." His thumb stroked the palm of her hand. "Let's talk about something more interesting. Why on earth did you become a detective?"

"I drifted into it by accident. I solved a few cases and then decided to set up my own agency." Agatha gave him several highly embroidered descriptions of cases she had worked on.

By the time the meal was over, Agatha felt herself sinking into the warm bath of obsession again. Everything about Sylvan fascinated her—his lean figure, his very Frenchness.

Outside the restaurant, she suggested they take a cab because they had drunk quite a lot, but Sylvan only laughed and said he was an expert driver.

As they drove down into Carsely, Agatha's heart was beating hard as she checked over her body. Legs and armpits shaved, check; condoms in the bedside table, check; toenails cut, check . . .

"Did you leave all the lights on?" asked Sylvan as he drew up outside Agatha's cottage.

"No," said Agatha. "Oh, snakes and bastards, it must be Charles. He has a key. I'll soon get rid of him."

She anxiously hurried to get out of the bucket seat of the sports car and tumbled out on the ground.

Sylvan laughed as he helped her to her feet. "Ah, the penalties of age," he said, and Agatha felt just as if he'd thrown cold water over her.

She opened the door and marched into the sitting room to find not only Charles but James.

Charles leaped to his feet and kissed Agatha on the cheek. "Have a nice time, darling?" he asked. "I've put my stuff in the bedroom. Thought I'd stay for a bit. James has come to say goodbye. He just got back today but he's off again tomorrow. Hullo, Sylvan. Police let you out, did they?"

Sylvan for a moment looked furious. Then he laughed easily and said, "I was never in police custody. Excuse me."

He drew Agatha back into the hall and whispered, "You should have told me you had a lover."

"He's not my lover," muttered Agatha fiercely. "I'll get rid of him."

"No, chérie, it doesn't matter. I am going to France with my boat in two days' time but I will be back a week on Saturday. Why not join me in Hewes on the Sunday for lunch and we will make up for lost time? I'll meet you at the Chinese restaurant at one o'clock." He took her in his arms and kissed her passionately.

"Yes, I'll see you there," croaked Agatha when she could. "But can't you stay? You can't go all the way back to Hewes tonight."

"I'll be fine. Bye."

Agatha stood on the doorstep and watched him roar off into the night.

Then she went back inside to confront James and Charles.

But James forestalled her by saying icily, "Have you run mad? There have been three murders down there and Sylvan Dubois must be involved in some way. Are you going to believe that he and the Bross-Tilkingtons are entirely innocent?"

"I'll bet he was only trying to seduce you to shut you up," said Charles.

Overwrought, Agatha, not usually given to swearing, told them both to go and perform impossible physical acts on themselves and stalked upstairs to bed.

Later, when she lay awake, she heard Charles coming up the stairs to go to the spare room. She thought he might come into her room to argue with her, but his door closed behind him and then there was silence.

At last, Agatha's anger died down as she began to feel obscurely that she'd had a lucky escape.

•   •   •

When she went into the kitchen in the morning, Charles was playing on the floor with her cats. He looked up at her and smiled. "Still mad at me?"

"How did you find out?" asked Agatha.

"James saw you leave and called on Mrs. Bloxby and then called on me to save you from a fate worse than death."

"I can take care of myself," said Agatha, lighting a cigarette.

Charles stood up, poured himself a cup of coffee, and said, "I was listening at the door. I heard him say he was going to France and would be back a week on Saturday and would see you on Sunday."

"So what? Are you going to follow me down to Hewes?"

"I've an idea. I think he's smuggling something. We could go to the port, Hadsea, hire a boat and go upriver and lurk on the other side of the stream from the Brosses' property and see if he brings anything in during the night on the Saturday before he's due to meet you."

"Not another boat!" Agatha told Charles about her adventures in the dinghy.

"No, no," said Charles soothingly. "We'll get something ferociously high-powered. I've got friends in Hadsea. I'll phone and see what I can get fixed up."

"Why this sudden enthusiasm for detection?" asked Agatha. "I felt sure you were chasing some girl."

"Me? No, just sloping around," said Charles. His

beautiful Tessa had wanted to go to a rock concert. Charles endured a weekend of noisy bands, pouring rain, mud and the determined cheering and enthusiasm of Tessa. Love died in him when he found the communal toilets blocked up and when Tessa told him not to be such a wimp and find a convenient hedge.

Hadsea was a small fishing port at the mouth of the river Frim. To her relief, the sea was calm. On Saturday Charles helped her board a large motor cruiser. "This can do forty-four knots," he said proudly.

"Have you checked about the currents in the river?" asked Agatha uneasily.

"I checked. I've got the maps. I know where the currents are. There's even a saloon with a bar. Go below if you like and I'll shout for you when we're nearly there. Borrowed it from friends. They're as rich as anything."

They must be, thought Agatha, as she went into the expensively appointed wood-panelled saloon. There was a bar in the corner. She poured herself a large gin and added tonic as the powerful engines began to roar. Agatha was determined to stay where she was until they arrived at their destination. She did not like boats. On a coffee table was a selection of magazines. She picked them up and flipped through them, reflecting it was surely a sign of age when she did not recognize many of the celebrities. Of course, with the advent of reality TV, it was possible to become a celebrity without really having done anything, studied acting, or achieved anything amazing in sport.

She was perfectly sure they would not find out anything sinister about Sylvan. She deserved a little fling, she told herself. It was all very well to be moral about casual sex, but when it turned out to be a long time since one had had any at all, morals became weak and shifting. Besides, by now the British police would have been in contact with the French police, and if there had been anything criminal about Sylvan, he would have been arrested.

The saloon was warm and comfortable and she was tired after the long drive and drifted off to sleep, only awakening when she heard Charles hailing her and realized the engines had stopped.

She climbed up and joined him, staring at all the gleaming instruments. "It looks like the cockpit of the Concorde," she said. "Where are we?"

"A little downriver and under the trees on the opposite bank. It's as dark as pitch. Now we wait. There's no sign of any boats at the jetty."

"When do you think he'll come?"

"Maybe soon. It's just after midnight. Now, think about this, Aggie. If he were an innocent yachtsman, he'd have come earlier."

"What if he's decided to come back by plane, car or train?"

"Always uses his boat. It's called *Jolie Blonde*. He's a great favourite down at the harbour. Always presents for the customs people at Christmas and a big donation to the local lifeboat. Doesn't that strike you as suspicious?"

"He might just be a very generous man. He's got a lot of money. Not all men are such tightwads as you, Charles."

"Miaow!"

Agatha stifled a yawn. "So we sit here all night?"

"I'll do a deal with you. When it gets up till two or three in the morning, we'll call it quits. Listen!"

It was a very still night, and faintly in the distance they could hear the throb of an engine.

A large cruiser painted some dark colour sailed up to the jetty and the engines were cut. A tall dark figure made the boat secure and then went below.

"Damn," muttered Charles. "Don't tell me he's going to spend the night on his boat."

They waited impatiently. "There's a lot of banging and moving going on," said Charles. The tall dark figure they guessed was Sylvan reappeared and said something. Six smaller dark figures climbed from the boat and stood on the jetty.

Charles nipped to the front of his boat where there was a powerful lamp and shone it straight on the group on the jetty. Sylvan's startled face stared into the light. Beside him stood six Chinese men.

Sylvan untied the tender and leaped back into his boat. A roar of engines and he shot off down the river.

"Chase him," yelled Agatha.

"No, phone the police. They'll alert Hadsea. And get them to pick up those poor sods. I hate this. They probably gave Sylvan their life savings to get smuggled in."

Agatha phoned the police and then they waited. The Chinese stood patiently. "They're waiting for someone," said Agatha. "I bet it's the owner of that Chinese restaurant. He probably moves them on to work as slave labour somewhere."

At last they could hear police sirens. "Lights are going on in the house," said Agatha. "The Brosses must be at home. They must be involved in this."

A police launch was the first to arrive. Then Jerry Carton appeared, shouting to his dogs as police cars roared down the grass on the riverbank.

"And do you think we'll get any thanks for this?" complained Charles. "Not a bit if it. They'll be on board soon. We'll need to go into the police station at Hewes and they won't believe in my lucky guess for a minute. They'll think we've been withholding information."

They were interviewed separately. Detective Superintendent Walker, flanked by Boase, was in a high temper. He said he was sure they knew all about the smuggling and instead of informing the police had decided to play at being detectives. His temper was further inflamed by the news that Jerry had escaped.

"May I remind you, I am a detective," complained Agatha, "and without us you'd have got sweet damn-all. I suppose you've arrested Bross-Tilkington."

"No, why? As far as we can gather, he had nothing to do with this."

"You must have lost your wits. George's best friend is unloading Chinese at the bottom of his garden and he doesn't know anything about it? What about his security-dog man?"

"Jerry Carton has disappeared. We are looking for him. We are also interrogating Mr. Bross-Tilkington, but he seems genuinely bewildered. It was Mr. Dubois who suggested hiring Jerry and then Sean."

"Well, I'm sure when you bring Sylvan Dubois in, he will inform you that they were all in cahoots."

Walker's eyes flickered uneasily and he glared down at notes on the desk in front of him.

"You've lost him!" exclaimed Agatha. "You've let him get away."

"He got out into the Channel but the coastguard will soon pick him up," said Walker heavily. "Now, if we can get back to the questioning . . ."

· · ·

Later the following morning, when Agatha and Charles, who had slept on their boat, woke up, Agatha phoned Patrick to ask him if his contact in Hewes could come up with any news. Patrick had heard about the hunt for Sylvan on the radio news that morning. "They've a fat chance of catching him," he said.

"Why?" asked Agatha. "They've got the coastguard out looking for him."

"Don't the cops down there read the newspapers? Coastguard staff around Britain are on a twenty-four-hour walkout over pay. It started at seven o'clock last night."

Agatha groaned. The thought of a surely vengeful Sylvan escaping frightened her.

When she rang off, she told Charles. Then she asked him, "What made you so sure he would be smuggling something?"

"It was because of something I read earlier this year," said Charles, nursing a mug of coffee. "In February, the police broke up a massive people-smuggling gang. Chinese people pay up to twenty-one thousand pounds to be smuggled into Britain. People like Sylvan are probably responsible for the France-to-Britain leg of the journey. That costs each five thousand pounds. In one flat in Peckham High Street in London, people found twenty-three Chinese living in cramped conditions. The police say it's a myth to think they're poor peasants. A lot of them are highly skilled."

"So what happens to them?"

"They think a lot get swallowed up by the restaurants in London's Chinatown."

"There's a Chinese restaurant here," exclaimed Agatha. "That's where Sylvan was going to take me for dinner. But I wonder how he got them in?"

"He was friendly with all the authorities down at Hadsea," said Charles. "I told you that. He probably had a room hidden somewhere in that large boat of his."

Agatha's phone rang. It was Patrick. "They're taking the Bross-Tilkington house apart this morning," he said, "but George is swearing innocence and they can't so far find a thing against him. They believe he was conned by Sylvan. They think maybe Felicity knew about it and was going to talk and that's why Sylvan shot her. George and his wife were flattered because Sylvan treated them royally when they were in Paris and introduced them to all sorts of famous people."

"Idiots," commented Agatha sourly.

"Oh, really? If it hadn't been for me, sweetie, you'd have got laid and into a blind obsession."

Agatha was saved from replying as a voice hailed them. Charles went up on deck. He came back down and said, "There's a police car on the pier. We're wanted back at the station."

•   •   •

Agatha was interviewed again by Boase and Walker. The detective chief superintendent's eyes were red-rimmed with lack of sleep. The police were still suspicious as to why Charles had leaped to the conclusion that Sylvan was smuggling something. "There is a detective-sergeant at Mircester who claims that you have withheld vital information in the past," said Walker severely.

"That will be a bitch called Collins," said Agatha wearily. "She hates me. I have helped Mircester police many times in the past."

Falcon put his head round the door. "A word, sir? It's urgent."

Walker told the tape the interview was being suspended and then left the room. He returned shortly, his eyes gleaming with excitement.

"Found something?" asked Agatha eagerly.

"Never mind. Wait outside until your statements are typed up, sign them and then you are free to go."

Agatha joined Charles in the small reception area. "Something's happened," she said. "Walker looked so excited, I believe they've got him."

"We'll wait to sign our statements," said Charles, "and then we'll get back to the boat and you phone Patrick."

"When did you learn to handle a boat?" asked Agatha. "I've been meaning to ask you."

"I was in the navy as a young man."

"Charles! I never ever think of you as doing anything useful."

A gust of wind rattled the windowpanes of the station. "Just as well I have," said Charles. "Seems to be blowing up."

After a quarter of an hour they were both called into a side room where they signed their statements. Then they went out into Hewes High Street, leaning against the increasing force of the wind.

"Do we have to go back to Hadsea today?" pleaded Agatha.

"'Fraid so. I promised to have it back. It's only a river, Agatha. It's not as if we have to go into the open sea."

Agatha kept to the saloon as the powerful boat set off downstream. She could feel all her self-confidence leaking out through her fingertips. She remembered with shame bragging to Sylvan about her great detective work. Was she really any good? Or was she surrounded by clever people like Charles? The sheer folly of going out on a date and accepting another with a Frenchman who had been at the scene of every murder was silly, to say the least.

Maybe she wasn't any good at being a detective at all. Maybe she just bumbled round like a trapped bee against a windowpane until someone opened the window and she saw daylight.

When they got to Hadsea and handed over the boat, Charles volunteered to drive them back as they had both come in Agatha's car, and a weary and demoralized Agatha sank down into the passenger seat.

"Before we drive off," she said, "I'd better phone Patrick and see why my interview was cut short."

Patrick said that a fishing boat had located Sylvan's boat adrift in the Channel and was towing it into Dover Harbour. An RAF patrol had been alerted earlier by the fishing boat's captain and had immediately flown over the area. They had seen Sylvan diving off into the sea. He hadn't been wearing a life jacket. They had circled over the *Jolie Blonde*. Sylvan had struck out for a little bit and then had sunk under the waves. They were now searching to see if the body surfaced.

Agatha relayed the news to Charles. "That's the end of that," he said.

"I don't know about that," said Agatha, stifling a yawn.

"Oh, come on, Aggie. It stands to reason. He'd slept with Felicity. She must have known something."

"But he had a cast-iron alibi."

"Did Patrick say whether the Bross-Tilkingtons are still being regarded as innocent?" asked Charles.

"Evidently so. The police feel they were being simply used all along the way. The security and the hiring of Jerry Carter were all Sylvan's idea. He frightened them to death with stories of burglars."

"So, end of chapter. Good," said Charles. "We can all get back to normal."

"What's normal?" mumbled Agatha and fell asleep.

She did not awaken until they were drawing up outside her cottage. "I'm starving," said Charles. "Let's see to your cats and then walk up to the Red Lion. Has John got his outside bit?"

"Last heard."

John Fletcher, landlord of the Red Lion, was lucky in that he'd had an extensive car park at the back. Half was now set out with tables and umbrellas enclosed in a heavy sort of plastic tent. The day was fine, so the sides had been rolled up. They ate a hearty meal and walked slowly back.

"My time to sleep," said Charles. "Care to join me?"

"The usual answer."

"You'll crack one of these days."

"Not me. I'd better go into the office. See you later."

Everyone except Mrs. Freedman was out. Agatha sighed and sat down at her computer to check through all the cases logged on it. "Nothing on that girl who went missing—Trixie Ballard?"

"Not a sign yet. Sharon's been working on it."

Agatha studied the notes on the case on her computer. The disappearance of the fifteen-year-old had received extensive coverage in the press. She looked up. "Did the parents appear on television?"

"Yes," said Mrs. Freedman. "If you Google BBC News and check back, you'll get it."

When the video link came up on the screen, Agatha turned up the sound on her speakers and listened carefully. Mrs. Ballard was a thin dyed blonde who sobbed uncontrollably. Mr. Ballard did all the talking, "Please come home, princess," he said, his voice breaking with emotion. "We miss you and we love you."

"That's odd," said Agatha when the brief video had finished. "He never appealed to anyone who might be holding her to let her go. Where is Sharon's report? No, don't worry. It'll be here somewhere."

Agatha found Sharon's report and studied it carefully. Sharon had been very thorough. School friends and teachers had been questioned along with next-door neighbours and local shops. She had left school two weeks ago to go home and seemed to have disappeared into thin air.

Still smarting at what she felt were her inadequacies as a detective, Agatha decided to see what she could find out about the girl herself.

The Ballards lived in a five-storey block of flats off a roundabout on the Evesham Road out of Mircester. It all looked very respectable, with private parking, no graffiti, and a tiny mowed piece of grass and flower beds along the edge of the car park.

Agatha was about to get out of the car when a thought struck her. Surely the parents, neighbours and friends would all just say the same thing. The girl's room would have been thoroughly searched. She remembered from the notes, Trixie's computer had been studied in case some paedophile had been grooming her.

Leaning back in the car, Agatha lit a cigarette and brought the faces of the parents up into her mind's eye. The father's face had looked bloated. Grief or drink?

A memory from her own childhood surfaced in her mind. Her parents had both been alcoholics. One night she had awakened to find her father standing at the end of her bed. "Move over, darling," he'd said.

And young Agatha had opened her mouth and screamed the place down. Her mother had come tottering in and her parents had ended up having a vicious fight.

Had daddy tried anything on with young Trixie? Now, if you were a fifteen-year-old, would you commit suicide? There was a lot of that around. But the reports had her down as a sensible girl, fairly good at exams.

What would I do? wondered Agatha.

With all the influx of immigrants from Eastern Europe, lousy jobs were hard to find, the sort of jobs where they didn't bother about employment details. She hoped Trixie hadn't gone to London, where there were plenty waiting to prey on runaways and put them into prostitution.

She was an ordinary-looking girl, tall for her age, with mousy hair. But if she dyed her hair and wore glasses, she could change her appearance.

What would I do? thought Agatha again. She lit another cigarette.

Work? Chambermaid or dishwasher. That might be it. Maybe not too far away. The report said she had never been out of Mircester before. She was too tall and not nearly pretty enough to attract a paedophile. She could pass for seventeen or eighteen.

She returned to the office in time for the evening briefing. "Sharon, you've done very good work on this girl, Trixie Ballard," said Agatha. "But I've got a feeling there might be trouble with the father. I don't think she's been snatched, and from that report from the school counsellor, she doesn't seem the suicidal type. It's a wild guess, but she might be working somewhere where they aren't too fussy about employment legalities. I want you all to take tomorrow to check hotels for chambermaids and restaurants for dishwashers. Jobs like that."

After briefing them, Agatha went wearily home. Charles had left. She fed the cats and let them out into the garden. She would start work on the Trixie case in the morning.

•　　•　　•

Toni had enjoyed her brief time of being her own boss. She felt she'd taken a great step backwards to be working for Agatha again. She was grateful to Agatha—too grateful—for all the help she had given her.

Most of the girls she had been to school with had settled for unexciting jobs. Still, thought Toni, they might turn out to be a good source of information as to low-paid jobs where too many questions might not be asked. Toni had opted to search the hotels. Trixie would need somewhere to stay.

Toni began by calling at Mircester's main supermarket. She walked right around the back of the building to where she knew the staff often stood outside, having a smoke.

Two of her old school friends were there. A thin, scrawny, spotty girl called Chelsea hailed her. "If it isn't our famous tec. What you doing, babes?"

"I'm looking for Trixie Ballard. Seen anything of her?"

Her companion Tracy, small and fat with lank hair, jeered, "Oh, sure. With all the cops in Britain looking for her?"

"Just wondered," said Toni and walked hurriedly away. She realized if she had begun to question them about hotels where Trixie might have found work, they would gossip all over the supermarket and if Trixie was in hiding in one of the hotels, she might get to hear of it.

The time to hit the hotels would be just after ten o'clock, when guests would be expected to vacate their rooms. At the posher hotels it would be midday. At least Mircester was only a market town. A big city like London or Manchester would be a nightmare.

She checked her list. There were five hotels. The George was the biggest but she couldn't imagine them employing someone without a social security number.

Then there was the Palace—same thing. The Country Inn was a possibility.

She went round to the staff entrance. A woman in a white overall came out and dumped rubbish in one of the bins and went in again. Toni went off and bought a white overall, put it on, returned to the Country Inn and boldly walked in by the service entrance and up the stairs.

She went up and down stairs and along corridors, checking into rooms where the maids were working but could not see any sign of anyone who looked like Trixie. In fact, most of the voices she heard sounded like Polish.

Toni finally gave up and went back to her car. Two hotels left, the Berkeley and the Townhouse. The Berkeley was actually a motel out on the ring road. That seemed the more hopeful of the two.

It was built like an E with the central bar missing. All she had to do was park in the courtyard to get a clear view of the maids coming in and out as they worked on the various rooms.

Not one of them looked like Trixie. Without much hope, she drove to the Townhouse. It was a small seedy-looking hotel.

Time had passed and surely the rooms would have been cleaned. Toni drove to the side of the hotel where she had a good view of the service entrance and waited. By late afternoon, the maids began to check out. There were about six of them but no Trixie.

She checked into the office for the final briefing. "Maybe we'll give it one more morning tomorrow," said Agatha, "and then that's that."

Sharon caught up with Toni outside. "You're looking right dismal these days, Tone. Is it that fellow, Perry?"

"It's part that. He had the cheek to send me flowers and keep phoning. He's finally given up. The liar kept saying it was a setup and he'd never seen the woman before."

"What's the other thing?"

"I'd like to be my own boss again."

"You could ask Agatha," suggested Sharon. "'Member she originally offered to set you up?"

"I want to be totally independent of Agatha. After all she's done for me, I don't feel like taking on any more gratitude. And I wouldn't be free of her. She'd be round checking the books and giving unwanted advice."

"Tell you what," said Sharon. "There's a sloppy movie, *To You My Love,* on at the Odeon. It's a bit of a pinch of *Sleepless in Seattle.* We could grab a burger and then go there."

Toni grinned and put an arm around Sharon's chubby shoulders. "Sounds good to me."

Agatha watched them from the office window. Toni was

wearing a black T-shirt, short denim skirt with a broad belt slung low over it and flat sandals. The sun glinted on her fair hair. Sharon was in her usual ragbag of fashions, chattering away animatedly.

I wish I were as young as that, thought Agatha moodily. They're off, out for the night, and I'm going home to my cats.

The film did not have a strong enough plot to hold Toni's attention, although Sharon, clutching a giant tub of popcorn to her generous bosom, seemed enthralled. Toni remembered when things at home were bad with her drunken brother, she would often escape to the cinema.

She sat up straight and peered around her. Would a girl like Trixie do the same? Of course the poor girl could be lying dead in a ditch somewhere.

Before the end of the film, she whispered to Sharon, "I'll meet you outside."

Sharon gulped and nodded in agreement, tears running down her face, as she stared avidly at the screen.

Toni positioned herself outside. The movie had received bad reviews and the cinema had been only one third full.

She took out the photo of Trixie and studied it. The girl could change her appearance but she had a small black mole at the right-hand corner of her mouth. I'll focus on that, thought Toni.

And then, as people began to come out, Toni spotted a girl with a hood drawn over her head. She caught a glimpse of a little black mole. Sharon came up to her. "You miss a great ending . . . What?"

"I've seen Trixie," hissed Toni. "Let's follow her."

They hurried after the hooded figure. The girl walked to the marketplace and waited. A van drove up with GREEN FINGER NURSERIES painted on the side. Trixie got in and the van drove off.

Toni and Sharon raced to Toni's car. "I know that nursery," said Toni. "It's out on the Bewdley Road. We'll get there and see if we can get a better look at her and then we'll call the police."

They parked a little way away from the nursery and got out. "I must get a closer look," said Toni. They cautiously approached the garden nursery. The air was full of the sweet smell of flowers and plants. The van was parked outside a low bungalow. "You wait here," hissed Toni. "I'll creep up and look in at the window. I hope they don't have dogs."

Toni moved silently forward across the parking space in front of the bungalow. Behind the bungalow, long glass-covered sheds glistened in the moonlight.

She crouched down and peered in a window which was lit up. A man and woman and a girl were sitting at a kitchen table. The woman was pouring tea. Staring at the girl, Toni realized that if it hadn't been for that telltale mole, she might never have recognized Trixie. She was wearing glasses and her hair was dyed blonde.

Toni slowly backed away. When she joined Sharon, she said, "I'll call the police."

"We'll get no glory," said Sharon.

"But they may have abducted her, even though it doesn't look like that."

"You phone," said Sharon. "I'm going behind that hedge for a pee."

Once behind the hedge, Sharon took out her mobile phone where she had logged in the numbers of all the important newspapers and television companies and began to talk rapidly.

Toni had managed to get Bill Wong and had urged him not to bring the police with all sirens blaring or Trixie might escape.

Very soon the first of the police cars began to arrive. Toni met them at the corner of the road. "Go easy," she whispered to Bill. "I think Trixie might have had trouble with her father."

"You mean abuse?"

"Something like that."

"You stay there and leave the job to us."

It seemed to take a long time. Then the press arrived in numbers. "It was Toni here that found her," said Sharon proudly.

"And Sharon," said Toni loyally. They put their arms

around each other and stood smiling and flashes went off in their faces.

Then there was a press scrum as the bungalow door opened and Trixie was led out, her head concealed by a blanket. The couple were led out as well, but Toni noticed they were not in handcuffs.

Detective Inspector Wilkes approached the two girls and said curtly, "Come down to headquarters. You'll need to make a statement."

On the way there, Toni said urgently, "Phone Agatha. She'll want to be in on this."

"Why? She did nothing."

"She's the boss. Phone!"

Sharon sulkily pulled out her mobile phone and pretended to dial. "No reply," she said cheerfully.

"Did you leave a message?"

"I forgot."

"Well, do it now!"

Agatha was outside James's cottage. He was not at home. She went back to her own cottage and locked up. She went upstairs and undressed and showered and then decided to put a face pack on.

As she sat on the edge of her bed, waiting for the face

pack to harden, she suddenly noticed the red light blinking on the phone receiver, which meant she had a message.

She picked it up, listened impatiently to the well-modulated recorded voice of the operator telling her she had one message and then pressed button one.

It was Patrick. "I've just had a phone call from a contact. Toni's found that missing girl and the press are all over the place." Cursing, she ran to the bathroom and rinsed off the face mask, struggled into her clothes, rushed out of her cottage and into her car and set off for Mircester.

By the time she got to police headquarters, all she could do was wait in the reception area for Toni and Sharon to reappear.

Two hours went past and then Toni and Sharon came out, looking weary.

Agatha listened as Toni described how they had managed to find Trixie. When she had finished, Agatha said coldly, "You should have phoned me immediately."

"I did phone," said Sharon. "There wasn't time to phone earlier and Toni could have made a mistake."

Agatha immediately felt mean and petty. She must have missed Sharon's message. But surely the operator had said there was only one message and that had been from Patrick.

"It was good work," she said. "Are the parents delighted?"

"They're interrogating Mr. Ballard. Toni told me that it

seemed as if Trixie had run away because the father had been abusing her. The couple at the nursery thought she was seventeen years old and she said she was waiting for her employment card and that she was an orphan. So they set her to work in the nursery and gave her bed and board."

When they left headquarters, the press had increased in numbers. Agatha tried to make a statement but they called for Toni and Sharon. Biting her lip, Agatha stood aside and watched her two young detectives get all the glory.

When Agatha finally got home and stared in her bathroom mirror, she saw to her dismay that bits of face pack were sticking to her eyebrows and in the front of her hair.

She had always been the one before who had been blessed with these leaps of detective intuition, she thought. Agatha remembered how she had tried to grab the limelight outside police headquarters and curled up into a tight ball on her bed, trying to make herself as small as she felt.

Chapter Eight

DESPITE THE THREATENING recession, business was booming at Agatha's detective agency. The publicity given to the finding of Trixie had engendered a great deal of work. It was time to expand. A surprising number of policemen were anxious to get out of the force, fed up with government targets. If an officer did not achieve a good number of arrests he had little chance of promotion, which meant that the more ruthless were charging normally law-abiding citizens with every petty offence they could think of. They were also overburdened with paperwork. She hired two men in their forties, Paul Kenson and Fred Auster. Paul was thin, gangly and morose and Fred was chubby and cheerful. But they were both highly competent.

Only, Toni and Sharon were becoming increasingly upset. The interesting cases no longer came their way. Agatha had them both back to looking for missing pets.

Phil and Patrick were pleased with the newcomers because both were able to take a much-needed holiday.

Phil had decided to spend his holiday at home, working in his garden.

Autumn was creeping into the Cotswolds. The leaves on the lime trees were already beginning to turn and the harvest had been brought in. But the Cotswolds were enjoying the rare glory of an Indian summer and one Saturday morning Phil's white hair was bent over a flower bed when he became aware of being watched.

He straightened up and turned round. Toni stood there. "What a nice surprise," said Phil. "I made a jug of lemonade this morning. Let's sit in the garden."

Toni sat down in a garden chair in front of a metal wrought-iron table. When Phil came out of the kitchen door carrying glasses and a jug of lemonade, Toni said, "I can hear the faint sounds of a band."

"That'll be over at the pub. There's some sort of village fete going on."

"No Agatha?"

"I gather from Mrs. Bloxby that she seems to have lost

interest in village things. I'm glad to see you. Any particular reason for this visit?"

Toni accepted a glass of lemonade and sighed. "It's Agatha."

"Ah."

"You might have noticed that ever since I found Trixie and got all that publicity and she hired those two new men, I'm being given all the rubbish."

"Yes, I had noticed," said Phil awkwardly. "You should speak to her about it."

"I suppose I should. The fact is, I'm tired of being grateful to Agatha. She rescued me from home, found me a flat, has protected me and looked after me. If I complain to her, yes, she'll probably put me on to something decent, but she should *want* to without me prompting her."

"She doesn't have telepathic powers, you know. You have to speak to her."

"You know, she scares me."

"Well, she can be a bit scary but she's got a heart of gold. You are very young. Maybe she's jealous."

"Of course she's jealous. Maybe she has a reason to be. I told Sharon after we had found Trixie to phone her and Sharon said she had. But it turns out she didn't and as Sharon is a friend of mine, Agatha thought we were deliberately cutting her out."

"Would you like me to speak to her?" asked Phil.

"No, it's all right. I've been thinking for a long time about joining the police force. It's so frustrating having to interview people when you haven't really any official capacity. But Agatha would think I was being ungrateful."

"Talk to Bill Wong about it and then maybe talk to Mrs. Bloxby. Mrs. Bloxby's such a sensible, calming sort of lady."

"As I'm in the village, I may as well call on her now. Thanks for the lemonade."

"You'll find her at the fete. It's in the field behind the pub."

"What if Agatha's there?"

"Then just pluck up your courage and talk to her."

Mrs. Bloxby was standing wearily behind a table boasting the legend VILLAGE HANDICRAFTS.

"Oh, Miss Gilmour. How very nice to see you," said the vicar's wife. "Ah, here is Mrs. Jardine to relieve me. Let's go over to the refreshment tent and get some ice cream. Such an unusually hot day."

Once they had queued up and paid for small dishes of strawberry ice cream, Mrs. Bloxby led the way to a small table in a corner of the tent.

"Is Mrs. Raisin coming to join us?" asked Mrs. Bloxby.

"No, the reason I'm here is to ask your advice about Agatha."

"She is not in any trouble, I hope?"

"No, I am. Ever since I received all that publicity over the Trixie case, Agatha has been giving me all the unimportant work."

"Then you must talk to her. Mrs. Raisin is a friend of mine. I cannot discuss her behind her back unless she herself has a problem that I might be able to help with. You have a great deal of courage to go out on nasty cases and yet you cannot speak to your kind—very kind—employer!"

"Agatha is more terrifying than a nasty case."

"Now, that's enough! Have you spoken to anyone else about this?"

"I called on Phil Marshall before I came here."

"This is a small gossipy village. Mrs. Raisin will soon hear about your visit and she will ask Mr. Marshall why you called and I have no doubt he will tell her. You had better go and see Mrs. Raisin immediately."

Toni approached Agatha's cottage with lagging footsteps. She rang the bell, hoping that Agatha was out. But the lady herself answered the door.

"Toni! What a nice surprise. Come through to the garden."

When they were seated at the garden table, Agatha asked, "Is this a social call?"

"No," said Toni, staring down at her feet.

"Then what is it?"

"Why are you giving me all the unimportant cases?"

"Well, I have two new detectives, Paul and Fred, and I want to really try them out."

Toni raised her blue eyes and looked straight into Agatha's face. "I think ever since the Trixie case that you've become jealous of me."

She waited for the storm to break. But Agatha's reaction surprised her. Agatha sat very still, staring out at the Cotswold hills beyond the village. From the fete came the faint sounds of the village band.

Then Agatha heaved a deep sigh and said quietly, "Yes, of course, you're quite right."

"But why?"

"I hate not being photogenic," said Agatha. "Even if I'd broken the case, the photographers and reporters have only got to see you and they forget I exist. I'm sorry. I've not been myself recently."

"What's the matter?"

"Age, I suppose. They say the fifties are the new forties, but they don't know what they're talking about. Charles comes and goes, James treats me like a fellow, and Sylvan's only interest in me was to keep track of what I might be finding out. It's very lowering. Charles is really the one who caught Sylvan. It was his idea, you know. You were the one who found Trixie. So not only am I worried about losing my looks and any attraction I might have had, I'm beginning to doubt my worth as a detective."

"Do you want me to leave?" asked Toni.

"Good God, no! I'll make it up to you on Monday morning. Now, I'll get us a drink. What would you like?"

Toni asked for a vodka and tonic.

When Agatha went off to get the drinks, Toni felt trapped. How could she leave now after Agatha's amazing burst of self-honesty?

Agatha came back with the drinks and looked at Toni's troubled face. "Forget about it," she said gruffly. "You'd have felt better if I'd shouted at you and told you you were talking rubbish, now wouldn't you?"

Toni gave a reluctant laugh. "Something like that."

"So let's move on to something else. Sylvan's body hasn't been washed up anywhere and that bothers me. The police have pretty much closed the case, although they're still looking for Sylvan—but not very hard. They have decided that Felicity knew something about the smuggling and that's why she was shot. Yet, they have accepted that George Bross was gulled by Sylvan and is innocent. I can't see that. I really don't trust that man. I wish I could get to his wife, Olivia. She was keen to employ me but it was her husband who cut her off."

"The agency is running well," said Toni. "Why don't you go back to Hewes and see if you can catch Olivia when she's out shopping or something?"

Agatha brightened. "That's an idea. I just don't like to leave the whole case alone with so many unanswered questions."

"You'd better go in disguise," said Toni uneasily. "If Bross is a villain, you might be in trouble."

"I'll go as myself," said Agatha defiantly. "It might stir things up."

Before she set out on Monday morning, after announcing to her staff that she was leaving Toni in charge, Agatha was tempted to phone Charles. But she quickly rejected the idea. If anything were to be found out about this case, then she would find it herself.

She booked herself into The Jolly Farmer and then wondered where to start. Downboys was such a small village. Perhaps if she parked somewhere along the road leading from Downboys to Hewes, she might see Olivia driving past. The countryside, basking in the Indian summer that was also blessing the Cotswolds, looked much friendlier and less threatening than she remembered. She parked a little way outside Downboys under a stand of trees and waited.

The hours dragged by. She probably shops in the village, thought Agatha, stifling a yawn. By late afternoon, she returned to Hewes, deciding to drive up to Downboys after dark and see if there were any lights on in the house. It would be silly to waste any more time if Olivia and George were not at home.

After dark she drove slowly past the house. Lights were on at the downstairs windows.

Now what to do? wondered Agatha.

She drove a little farther and came to a stop again. She wondered if she phoned whether Olivia would answer. But if she called and George answered and she hung up, he might check to find out who had been phoning, recognize her number from before and then start chasing her all around Hewes, shouting at her not to interfere.

Still, she had come all the way to Downboys to see if she could stir something up. She took out her mobile after checking the phone number and dialled.

To her relief, Olivia answered. "This is Agatha Raisin here," said Agatha quickly. "Remember me? I just wondered how you were getting on."

"I have to speak to you," whispered Olivia.

"We can meet," said Agatha urgently. "I'm at The Jolly Farmer in Hewes."

"Ten o'clock tomorrow morning," said Olivia and rang off.

I might get something here at last, thought Agatha cheerfully. If Olivia is sure that Sylvan killed Felicity, then I'll be able to get back to Mircester and stop fretting about the whole thing.

. . .

Agatha waited the next morning. Ten o'clock came and went. She had been waiting in the hotel lounge but she went out into the street and waited there, looking anxiously to left and right.

By noon, she finally decided that something had happened. She got in her car and drove slowly in the direction of Downboys, studying approaching cars in case Olivia passed her on the road.

An ambulance raced past her heading in the Hewes direction. I hope that's got nothing to do with Olivia, thought Agatha.

She drove up to the house. The gates were shut. With Jerry Carton gone, she wondered if the other entrance would still be guarded. She drove round there. No one tried to stop her.

Agatha crossed the lawn towards the French windows, looking nervously to right and left in case the dogs were still around. She saw a woman pushing a vacuum cleaner in the sitting room. The windows were open.

The woman saw Agatha, switched off the machine, and asked, "What do you want?"

"Are you Mrs. Fellows?" asked Agatha, remembering the name of one of the cleaners Toni had interviewed.

"No, I'm Mrs. Dimity. There's nobody home. Mr. Bross has gone to the hospital with his wife."

"What happened?" asked Agatha.

"Poor lady fell down them stairs out in the hall and broke her jaw on the banisters."

"Do you know which hospital she is in?"

"Hewes General, I should suppose."

Agatha hurried back to where she had left her car. Did Olivia slip or was she pushed? She had to get in to see her.

At The Jolly Farmer, she wrote down instructions to the hospital. She found a medical supplies shop and bought herself a white lab coat and a stethoscope.

She drove to the hospital and parked. She struggled into the white coat. Luckily, she had a name tag in her handbag left over from a conference she had attended as part of a former case. She pinned the white plastic name tag to the lab coat, slipped her phone into one of the pockets, and then locked her handbag in the boot of the car.

With the stethoscope dangling around her neck, she made her way into the hospital. Agatha guessed that Olivia had probably been put into a private room. The trouble was, in order to look like an authentic member of staff, Agatha had to walk briskly up and down, all the time fearing she would be challenged.

At last, at the end of a corridor, she saw George coming out of a room. Agatha hurriedly backed into the nearest room.

"And about time, too," said a querulous old voice. "I've been ringing and ringing for that bedpan. Hurry up about it. I don't want wet sheets."

An elderly lady with sparse silver hair and a withered face was lying glaring at her. Agatha went into the bathroom and reluctantly picked up a bedpan. If she told the old lady it wasn't her job, then the old dear would start ringing that bell again.

Agatha went back into the room, pulled back the covers and slipped the bedpan under the old lady. It seemed to take forever and then a dreadful smell rose up. Agatha remembered seeing some moist tissue wipes in the bathroom. She came back with a bundle, eased the patient up and cleaned her, then carried the bedpan back to the bathroom. Shuddering, Agatha tipped the contents down the toilet, poured some disinfectant into the pan, and then hurriedly made her escape.

That's what's waiting for us all when we get old, thought Agatha. She walked along to the room she had seen George leaving and opened the door and went in.

Olivia was lying in bed with her eyes closed. Her jaw had been wired shut.

Agatha softly approached the bed. "Olivia," she whispered. "It's me. Agatha."

Olivia's eyes opened and she stared at Agatha in fright. One hand appeared from under the bedclothes and made shooing motions.

Agatha saw a pad of paper and a pen on the table beside the bed. She was about to write, "What happened?" but instead she wrote, "Where is Sylvan?"

And then George's voice could be clearly heard coming back along the corridor. "I'll just have a last look-in on my wife and see if she's comfortable."

Agatha darted into the bathroom and closed the door. The door did not have a lock but there was a stool for the elderly and infirm to use when sitting under the shower. She jammed it under the door handle and then pressed her ear to the door.

She heard a voice say, "I would leave your wife to sleep, Mr. Bross-Tilkington. She's had a bad shock and needs rest. I'm just going to give her a shot of sedative."

"Good idea. Make sure she has no visitors. Got it? Not one."

"Certainly. I will give instructions to the desk."

Agatha waited until she was sure they had gone, removed the stool, and went back into the hospital room. Olivia's eyes were closed but tears were running down her cheeks. "I can help you," whispered Agatha. She gave her the pad. "Quickly. Before the sedative kicks in."

With a great effort, Olivia wrote something and then fell back on the pillows.

Agatha ripped off the sheet of paper and hurried out. When she finally got into her car, she heaved a sigh of relief. She took the piece of paper out of her pocket and studied it. The spidery writing straggled across the page. Olivia had written, "Calle Miro, Ramblas, Barcelon . . ."

Agatha frowned. Was Sylvan still alive? She had always been sure he had escaped. It was no use going to the police with this information. George would say they spent their honeymoon in Barcelona. He would get Agatha charged with something or other.

She would need to go herself. She would tell her staff she needed a break. Toni would be left in charge to make up for her, Agatha's, lousy treatment of the girl. If it all turned out to be a load of rubbish which led nowhere, then everyone would believe she had simply been in Spain on holiday.

Agatha decided to spend another couple of weeks making sure the agency was running smoothly and then say she was going on holiday.

But someone really ought to know where she was and why she was going. It was dark when she drove down into Carsely. The church was illuminated, shining with a golden light, welcoming her home.

She decided if Charles was in her cottage, she would tell him and maybe persuade him to go with her. But her cottage was dark and silent, with only the patter of the cats' feet as they came to investigate.

Agatha desperately wanted to find out something all by herself, to prove to herself and others that she really was a good detective.

• • •

Agatha sat in an open-air café on the Ramblas in Barcelona and watched the crowds go up and down. She wondered if that's what most of them did on Saturday—walk up one way and then down to the port the other way. Earlier that morning, she had located Calle Miro, but it was a narrow street leading off the Ramblas, with tall apartment buildings on either side. She did not have a house number and there was no café where she could sit and look to see if Sylvan appeared, so she had settled on the Ramblas. If Sylvan—if he were alive—had bought a new boat, then surely he would head from his apartment down the Ramblas to the port.

Her eyes grew tired with watching the moving crowd. At last, she decided it might be better to go down to the port herself and study the yachts. With her sore hip seeming to make the walk very long, she pushed her way through throngs of people gathered around the living statues. She stopped to watch a man posing as a statue of Julius Caesar, wondering how he could manage to remain so motionless.

The sun was warm as she reached her goal and strolled along looking at all the yachts and motor cruisers.

By early evening, Agatha was beginning to feel tired, hungry and defeated. She found a restaurant and ordered a small jug of red wine and a plate of roast rabbit, noticing with pleasure the large glass ashtray on the table in front of her. Unlike the French and British, the Catalans were happy to flout the cigarette ban.

She decided to stay just one more day. Then she would take Olivia's scrawled note back to the police, although she would need to think up a good reason as to why she had kept it so long.

Fortified by a good dinner, she decided to take a taxi back up to the Calle Miro and take one last look around.

The tall buildings reared up on either side of the narrow street. It was hopeless, she decided after half an hour of gazing up at windows.

She turned away towards the Ramblas and was passing a dark alley when she was suddenly grabbed and a pad of something was thrust over her mouth. She kicked and struggled, feeling herself losing consciousness.

When Agatha came to, she opened her eyes cautiously. Her hands were bound behind her back with duct tape and her ankles were bound as well and she was wearing a bathing suit.

So this is it, thought Agatha, trying not to cry. I'm to be dumped at sea.

She was lying on her side. Apart from the bed on which she had been placed, there was only one hard chair and on the wall, a badly executed painting of the Virgin Mary.

Agatha felt nausea rising in her throat and rolled over to the edge of the bed and vomited violently on the floor.

The door opened and a woman came in. She had a gypsy appearance: swarthy skin, large brown eyes and masses of coarse dark hair.

She muttered something and came back with a bucket and mop and began to clean the floor. "Help me," croaked Agatha.

The woman continued mopping. Agatha stared at the painting and said desperately, "Madre de Dios."

The woman started, crossed herself, but left the room, carrying the bucket and mop with her.

Agatha drifted off into unconsciousness again. When she recovered, the room was dark. A solitary candle burned under the portrait of the Virgin. Agatha's face was stinging and burning. Chloroform, she thought bitterly. My face will be a mass of sores.

A light French voice sounded from the next room. "You know what to do, Maria. See to her."

Maria, the woman from before, came in carrying a syringe. She knelt before the Virgin and then approached the bed. "Please," whispered Agatha. "Por favor."

Maria put a finger to her lips and jabbed the syringe into the mattress and emptied it. She ripped the tape from Agatha's wrists and ankles. Then she gently closed Agatha eyes. "Dead," she whispered. "Like dead."

Agatha nodded.

Half an hour passed. Then she heard two men entering the room. She was lifted up and heaved over one man's shoulder. Then she heard Sylvan's voice. "The bitch weighs a ton."

"Get her out of here." George Bross! Surely that was George's voice.

Agatha found playing dead very hard as she was bundled into a sack and carried down a staircase, her legs bumping against the banister.

"Into the boot with her," ordered Sylvan.

She was thrown in and heard the boot lid slam down.

The car jolted and rumbled over cobbles. The journey did not seem to take very long. Then the boot was lifted and she smelled salt air.

Sylvan threw her over his shoulder again. "Is this the best you could manage?" she heard George say.

"We needed a cheap, anonymous-looking boat. This is it. Now get her out to sea, get her out of the sack and dump her. She'll be dead to the world for another few hours. I'll wait for you here."

Agatha felt the dip and sway as she was carried aboard a boat. Then down the stairs to the cabin, banging her head and feet as she was hauled down.

She was thrown on some sort of bunk, the sack was dragged off her and then she heard George retreating.

Agatha opened her eyes. She was lying in a squalid, smelly cabin. The engine started up. Agatha realized she was very weak and would have to get up on deck and jump over the side as soon as possible.

Terror was giving her strength. She staggered to her feet and lurched to the companionway. George was at the wheel and the roar of the engine stopped him from hearing her creeping up the stairs.

Agatha moved quietly away from him to the stern of the boat. Then she wondered whether she might be in danger of being caught up in the propeller. She moved back a bit and summoning up all her courage, threw herself over the side.

She gasped as she went down and took in a gulp of salt water. She kicked and surfaced. Her heart sank. The lights of the port seemed very far away and she did not think she had enough strength left to swim that far.

And then the water was lit up with one mighty explosion. The boat with George in charge had exploded in a ball of flame.

Agatha realized that Sylvan had planned to get rid of both of them. A police launch came racing out from the port, its strong headlight shining across the sea. Agatha waved frantically, treading water.

The launch curved round Agatha and soon strong hands were helping her on board. A policeman who spoke English was hurried forward to her. Agatha gasped and explained briefly what had happened and that Sylvan Dubois, wanted by Interpol, was alive.

And then, for the first time in her life, the redoubtable Agatha Raisin passed out.

Agatha awoke in a hospital bed in a private room. She struggled up against the pillows. Two Spanish detectives were sitting beside her bed. One said in English, "You must tell us quickly, what happened? We found the apartment in the Calle Miro but there was no one there."

Agatha wearily began at the beginning of her story, of how Olivia had given her the street name in Barcelona. She said she decided to investigate the matter herself. But she called Maria "Carmen," the only Spanish name she could think of, and gave the police a false description. She explained how she was supposed to be drugged and dumped at sea so that it would look like a swimming accident, or rather, that was what George Bross had been led to believe. Sylvan had really meant to kill them both. She was suddenly frightened that Sylvan might already be heading to England to deal with Olivia, but the detectives assured her that Olivia was now being guarded.

Then later that day, the Spanish detectives were replaced by English detectives from the Special Branch. She had to go through the whole story again. One detective said, "The press are clamouring outside. We're not against getting this in the newspapers because it will put everyone on the alert. We're offering a reward for the capture of Sylvan Dubois."

"Give me a mirror," ordered Agatha.

A nurse brought her a hand mirror and Agatha squeaked in horror. Her face was covered in red sores from the chloroform and her hair was lank and dull.

"I must have make-up," she cried. "And a hairdresser."

Agatha's story made all the television channels and all the newspapers in Europe and Britain.

Maria, back in a gypsy encampment high up in the Pyrénées, read Agatha's exploits and was glad she had escaped. She had been in love with Sylvan, besotted by him, right up until the evening when she realized he was a murderer.

Roy Silver felt sulkily that he could have done with some of that publicity and that Agatha should have taken him to Barcelona.

Charles and Mrs. Bloxby were appalled at how near death Agatha had been. Sitting in the vicarage garden, Charles said, "I saw Agatha on television last night and she looked so white-faced."

"That was probably thick make-up," said Mrs. Bloxby. "She said that she believed she was chloroformed and that burns the skin. I wonder where Mr. Lacey is?"

．　　　．　　　．

James was at that moment sitting beside Agatha's bed, giving her a lecture. "I could hardly believe my eyes when I read about you," he said. "You should have gone straight to the police."

"Oh, stop nagging," said Agatha. She was starting to feel more cheerful. "I was beginning to wonder about my detective abilities, but I have really proved myself."

"You were more like a tethered goat than a detective," said James. "Anyway, they say you can go home tomorrow, so I've decided to act as bodyguard."

"That's kind of you," said Agatha, studying his handsome face and wondering why she didn't feel a thing for him.

"Did Olivia say anything now? Does she know who killed her daughter?"

"She believes it was Sylvan. Evidently she genuinely knew nothing about the smuggling."

Agatha did not return to a hero's welcome from the police. Mircester was furious with her, as was Hewes. Thanks to a good lawyer supplied by James, she escaped being up in court on a charge of obstructing the police in an investigation.

Then she had to straighten out affairs at the agency. The

two new detectives, Paul Kenson and Fred Auster, had complained about anyone as young as Toni being the boss and had been refusing to take orders.

Agatha, rattled by her interview with the police, blasted them and threatened both of them with the sack and then sent them scurrying off to do the jobs they had previously refused. James was calling at the office in the early evening to take her out to dinner. Agatha was looking forward to being seen with a handsome man—but that was all.

Well, that *was* all until James graciously extended the invitation to include Sharon and Toni. Toni took one look at Agatha's face and said hurriedly that neither she nor Sharon was dressed to go out to dinner. But James was so insistent that Agatha felt obliged to urge them to join them.

Sharon had shaved her eyebrows and pencilled in two arches, giving her round face a look of surprise. She had also acquired a nose stud. Her red-dyed hair was streaked with blonde and her generous breasts slipped out of a low-cut blouse. Toni was wearing a faded T-shirt and jeans. But the pair of them were in high spirits and James smiled on them indulgently.

It was then Agatha wished she had a man of her own. James had turned into a sort of big brother, Charles came and went, and Roy made occasional visits. But someone of her very own by her side, thought Agatha dreamily, would mean company in her old age, would mean a protector as well, because the shadow of Sylvan was always there to haunt her.

"What are you thinking about?" demanded James suddenly.

"Oh, this and that," answered Agatha vaguely. But she had just remembered hearing about an exclusive dating agency. It cost of lot of money and catered to the rich. "I'll try that," said Agatha out loud.

"Try what?" asked Sharon.

"Something for dessert," replied Agatha.

Chapter Nine

A MONTH LATER, Agatha dressed with great care for her first date. It was all very exciting. She looked at the photo stuck on her dressing table mirror. It showed a slim man of middle height with thick brown hair and a pleasant smile. And he was none other than Baron, Lord Thirlham; hobbies, fine wines, reading, and country walks.

He had an estate in Oxfordshire and they had agreed to meet in the restaurant at the Randolph Hotel in Oxford.

Agatha was wrapped in a warm dream as she left for her date. She could see the announcement in the *Times*. She would be Lady Thirlham. She would give up the detective agency and become a real lady. She would open fetes and do good works. People would say how gracious she was. Thirlham was a widower. So much easier, surely, when the man had been married already.

After she had parked her car in the hotel car park, she made her way into the Randolph and through to the dining room.

"Lord Thirlham's table," said Agatha grandly to the maître d'.

She was ushered to a table at the window. She was exactly on time but his lordship had not yet put in an appearance. Agatha had planned to drink very little because she was sure she would be motoring home. The agency gave strict advice that couples should take time to get to know each other first. But a quarter of an hour passed and there was still no sign of the baron. Agatha ordered a stiff gin and tonic.

After another quarter of an hour had passed, she was just about to leave when a small round man was ushered up to the table. Agatha looked at him in amazement. "Lord Thirlham?"

"That's me," he said, sitting down and shaking out his napkin. He must have sent a photo of himself when he was younger, thought Agatha dismally. His hair was grey. His face was round with rather protruding eyes and a small pursed mouth. In fact, thought Agatha, he had probably sent in a photo of one of his friends.

He smiled at her and said, "The purpose of this dinner is

to find out about each other, so I will tell you all about my-self."

And so he did—in long, studied periods, pausing only from the fascination of his own life story to order food and wine. He began with his childhood, his nanny, his brother and two sisters, his school, university, army and yackety, yackety, yack, unaware that Agatha was no longer listening.

At last, Agatha could not bear it any longer. As the coffee arrived, she rose to her feet.

"Going to powder your nose?" he said.

"Sure."

Agatha made her way out to the desk and said to the concierge, "Could you tell the maître d' to bring my share of the bill. I wish to pay it now. Do not let my dining companion know I am leaving."

Payment completed, Agatha fled out into the night. She had paid a very large amount to the dating agency. They would certainly hear from her in the morning.

The agency was full of apologies. They pointed out that their contract stated that if Agatha had not met anyone suitable in a year's time, then two thirds of her money would be refunded.

Hope seemed to spring eternal in Agatha's bosom. Perhaps the next one would be the man of her dreams. She had told the agency that the next photograph she received must be a proper picture of her date.

For a time, it seemed as if no one on the agency's books found the idea of Agatha Raisin appealing. Then one morning she received a letter from the agency along with a photograph and description. Her next hopeful was a university lecturer. His photograph showed a tall thin man of her own age wearing glasses and dressed in a tweed jacket and flannels. He had a rather frog-like mouth. His name was John Berry. May as well give it a try, thought Agatha.

The meeting was to be in London at a restaurant in Chinatown. Agatha decided to take the train up to town. She was wearing a comfortable trouser suit and flat walking shoes. She planned to visit a hairdresser in London prior to the meeting because she always felt more confident with her hair just newly done.

Memories of Sylvan made her feel uneasy as she entered the restaurant. She could not help wondering how many of the staff had been smuggled into Britain.

She recognized her date from his photograph. He rose and gave her a charming smile. Agatha brightened.

Her brightness dimmed a little after she had sat down and he said cautiously, "You know the rules are that on our first date we should each pay for our own meals."

"Yes, of course," said Agatha.

He suggested they should order the cheapest set menu for two. Agatha wondered how he could afford to hire such an expensive agency. He was wearing the tweed jacket he had worn in the photo over an open-necked Hawaiian shirt.

"It says in your résumé," he began, "that you are a businesswoman. What kind of business?"

"I run a detective agency," said Agatha.

"You're a snoop!" he exclaimed.

"I am a private detective," said Agatha coldly. "People hire me to—"

His eyes flashed behind his thick glasses. "You snoop for the government," he said.

"I do not!"

"You lot always lie. It's because I organized the march to that nuclear power station."

"Rubbish."

"Don't you rubbish me. I bet my phone's tapped. You're just the type they would employ—some posh, rich bourgeois female."

"You are talking absolutely bollocks," shouted Agatha. "You're paranoid!"

"Don't you dare call me paranoid. I know you lot."

"Before I get up and walk out of here," said Agatha evenly, "just tell me why you hired this expensive agency to find you a mate?"

"Because my father died and left me a packet. I want someone of similar tastes to fight the fight with me."

Agatha took out her wallet and counted out the money to cover her half of the bill.

"Get stuffed," she roared and stood up and marched out of the restaurant.

That's definitely it, she thought. She had booked herself into a hotel for the night. She planned to go to the agency in the morning and give them a piece of her mind.

In the morning, she walked from her hotel to the Diamond Dating Agency in South Molton Street. She found the office in chaos. Two debutante-looking girls were packing files into boxes. One had obviously been crying. "Where is Amanda?" asked Agatha, remembering the name of the owner.

"Gone bankrupt," said one of the girls. "Just like that. We're to pack up and get out."

"What? I want my money back," roared Agatha. "Where is Amanda Carlson?"

"She's most horribly upset. She's at her house."

"And where is her house?"

"It's at Kynance Mews in Kensington. Just along beside the vet's place."

Agatha took a taxi over to Kensington, marched down the mews and rang the bell at Amanda's door. A curtain upstairs twitched but no one came to answer the door.

Agatha shouted through the letter box: "Open this door or I'll make such a scene all your neighbours will know about your bankruptcy."

She heard footsteps descending the stairs inside. The door opened and Amanda stood there. She was a handsome woman in her forties with an hourglass figure and sculpted hair.

"Oh, it's you," she said bleakly. "I might have known. Come in."

Agatha followed her into a downstairs living room. Her quick eye took in what she privately thought of landlord's "posh" furnishings: pseudo mini country house.

"You don't even own this place," complained Agatha. "And I want my money back. I must have been mad. Ten thousand pounds and so far all I've met are a couple of freaks."

"I am sorry. I haven't any money."

"I bet you have. You're the sort that hides cash away from the income tax. You either get it or I will go straight to the newspapers."

"You bitch!" hissed Amanda. "Wait here."

Agatha waited impatiently. At last Amanda came down the stairs and handed her a packet of notes. "It's all there," she said sulkily.

Snatching the packet and stuffing it in her handbag, Agatha went out and slammed the door behind her.

It was only after she had collected her car from the car park at Moreton-in-Marsh station and was driving down to Carsely that she realized she should have asked for her file back and insisted that all her details be erased from the computer at the agency.

But she was reluctant to make the long journey back. She was also strangely reluctant even to phone. Agatha felt like a fool. She went to see Mrs. Bloxby instead and told that lady for the first time of her futile attempts to find a mate.

Mrs. Bloxby was tempted to burst out laughing at Agatha's descriptions of the two men she had met, but Agatha looked so upset, she didn't dare. When Agatha had finished, she said quietly, "Did you not check out the agency first?"

"I should have done, but it seemed so respectable. It was right near where I used to have my office. They advertised in all the main glossy magazines. I got my money back. I'd better put it down to experience and just get back to work."

"Is getting a man so important to you, Mrs. Raisin? I always thought of you as being self-sufficient."

Agatha sighed. "It would be great to have someone to go on holiday with, to have someone at the end of the day to talk over cases."

"Sometimes someone appears when you least expect it," said Mrs. Bloxby. "Mr. Lacey was looking for you yesterday."

"Oh, what did *he* want?"

"I suppose he just wanted to talk to you."

"I can't ever look at him the same way again," said Agatha. "First he ends our marriage because he wants to be a monk. Then he decides to get engaged to a girl nearly half his age and almost *flaunts* her in front of me. I feel nothing for him now."

"But you used to discuss things with him. Has there been any sighting of Sylvan?"

"Nothing, last heard."

Agatha went back to her cottage. She dug some fish out of her freezer and defrosted it before cooking it for her cats. They had barely touched the hard food she had left for them.

Then she went next door and rang James's bell. He opened the door and smiled at her. "I was looking for you yesterday."

"I was up in town," said Agatha. She followed him in and sat down on the sofa.

"Coffee?"

"Drink."

"Okay. I suppose it's a G and T. But don't smoke!"

When he came back with her drink, he asked, "No news of Sylvan?"

"Not a thing."

"Are you absolutely sure that Olivia knows nothing?"

"The police seem pretty sure. I wonder if she's got any money of her own, because the police will want to seize what they can, claiming the house and everything were the results of crime."

"It might be an idea to go and see her. I'll come with you, if you like."

Agatha groaned. "I can hardly bear the thought of that long journey to Downboys."

"I'll drive."

"All right. Tomorrow, though. I'd better get into the office and see how things are going."

Downboys looked every bit as bleak as Agatha remembered it to be. They drove to the house. But there was a FOR SALE sign outside and no one was at home.

They went to the pub and asked if anyone knew where Olivia had gone. A woman said that Olivia had gone to stay with her sister in Brighton and Mrs. Fellows or Mrs. Dimity, her former cleaners, might have the address.

Mrs. Fellows found the address after a long search. "It's in number five, Beau Square, near the Steyne."

"Well, it's not too far to Brighton," said James.

Does he feel nothing? wondered Agatha, studying his profile. We were married, we made love, and yet here we are like a couple of old bachelors.

Beau Square was actually not a square but a cul-de-sac with pretty little painted houses fronting on the cobbled street.

A stout grey-haired woman answered the door. "We wish to speak to Olivia?" said Agatha.

"Are you from the press?"

"No, here is my card. Olivia knows me."

"Wait there," she said, slamming the door in their faces.

She was gone so long that they began to fear that Olivia was not going to see them, but the door eventually opened and they were ordered inside.

Olivia was in a pleasant downstairs living room. She had lost weight but she seemed composed.

"This is my sister, Harriet," said Olivia, introducing them. "Harriet, Agatha was the detective I once hired to try to find out what happened to my dear daughter. James was engaged to her."

"I remember you from the wedding," said Harriet, fixing James with a cold eye. "Too old for her by half, that's what I thought."

"Please sit down, both of you," said Olivia. "Could you give us a minute or two, Harriet?"

Harriet stomped out. Olivia sighed. "My sister is very protective of me."

"We wondered," said Agatha, "if you knew why on earth Sylvan would kill your daughter on her wedding day?"

"The trouble is," said Olvia, "the police still can't figure out how he did it. He had a perfect alibi."

"Do you think your daughter knew about the smuggling and said something—like, she would tell her new husband?"

"My daughter was an innocent, through and through. Just a child, really. My husband and I had separate bedrooms and sometimes she would come into my bedroom at night and ask me to read her a story, just like she used to do when she was little. The police think Sylvan hired someone to kill her."

"What I can't understand, Olivia," said Agatha, "is how you could not possibly think something criminal was going on?"

"How could I? George made so much money from real estate in Spain. He said he loved his boat. I get seasick, so I was happy when he went off on his own or with Sylvan. Sylvan! I still find it hard to believe. We were both dazzled by him. Felicity wanted to get married. A white wedding was her great dream. She was quite childlike. The headmistress at her school said she was a trifle retarded. But she was so sweet. She cost George a fortune getting her whole appearance altered. Liposuction, the best plastic surgeon in California, personal trainer, everything of the best. Sylvan said men never noticed a woman had no brains provided she was beautiful."

James flushed dark red. "Sylvan said an older man was just what she needed. When I think of it, all he did was pull the strings like a puppet master," said Olivia. "I've cried and cried until I can't cry anymore. Do you think they will ever find Sylvan?"

"I hope so," said Agatha. "My great fear is that he'll find me first. Do you miss your husband?"

"I don't know. He became such a bully. I got so used to being shouted at and ordered around, it feels strange—empty, somehow. I can't really think of him. I'm sorry he had to die so terribly but to think he was still consorting with the man who may have got my daughter killed . . ." Harriet came into the room and said gruffly, "You'd better leave."

"I feel that was a wasted journey," said James, as they took the long road home.

"Not really," said Agatha. "I don't think Olivia is any sort of actress. I think she's a bit simple herself. I feel a loose end has been tied up."

"What about dinner when we get back?" suggested James.

"All right. But just the pub will do."

"You can't smoke, you know."

"Oh, yes, I can. He's got patio heaters."

Charles turned up and joined them for dinner. It was an easy, companionable meal. What on earth would today's feminists make of me? thought Agatha. They would point out that I have a successful business and friends. Why do I need a man? Sex. Well, they would point out, sex is easily come by. But it's love I want, thought Agatha. It's love that causes the high and fills up the brain with golden thoughts so that one feels invulnerable. It's love that makes all the tiresome maintenance of a middle-aged woman easy.

But one thing she had learned the hard way: No more dating agencies.

After a few weeks, Agatha received a letter with the heavily embossed heading ARISTO DATING. They said they had taken over the premises of the Diamond agency. Diamond had sold them their list of clients. Would Agatha like her details erased? If not, they could introduce her to some very suitable men. There would be no fee unless she found someone she liked.

Hope again sprang in Agatha's bosom, although a voice of common sense was telling her to forget it. But Christmas was slowly approaching. She did not want to be alone.

She conjured up a vision of a tall handsome man who owned a pleasant country mansion with dogs and wood fires. They would go for long walks and return in the evening to a companionable dinner. And then later, they would walk up the stairs to the master bedroom hand in hand, and he would say . . .

"I've finished, Agatha," called her cleaner, Doris Simpson. The bubble of Agatha's dream burst as she went to pay Doris. But the dream came back during the day.

She finally e-mailed the agency and said any man they considered suitable should e-mail her along with a photograph.

A reply came the following day. His name was Geoffrey Camden. He was tall and rangy with thick grey hair. He was standing on the steps of a country mansion with two gun dogs at his heels. He wrote that he was a widower who liked shooting, fishing and visits to the London theatres. He had seen her photograph and read her details.

Agatha thought that Mrs. Bloxby would probably tell her to forget the whole thing, but she felt she had to talk to someone. It was Sunday evening. She phoned the vicar's wife who said immediately that she would call round. "Alf is always like a bear with a sore head by Sunday evening," she said. Alf was her husband and Agatha felt that by Sunday evening, the vicar should have been feeling spiritually uplifted.

Mrs. Bloxby sank down gratefully on the soft feather

cushions of Agatha's sofa, accepted a glass of sherry, and asked, "What's been happening?"

Agatha had printed off the e-mail. She showed it to her.

"I think you had better check up on him first and find out if he is who he says he is," said Mrs. Bloxby. "If he's got a mansion, he might be in *Who's Who*. Do you have a copy?"

"It's about five years old. Wait. I'll get it."

Agatha came back with the book and searched the pages. "Well, I'm blessed. Here it is. Retired army major. Widower. Address, The Grange, Abton Parva, Shropshire. Hobbies—just like the ones in the e-mail. Age fifty-five."

"Maybe you should go up to London first and check out this agency. Sniff out if they're competent."

"I think I'll continue to e-mail him for a bit. I didn't put down 'detective' in my CV for the last agency. I'll tell him and if that doesn't put him off, maybe I'll take a chance."

By the end of two weeks of e-mails, Agatha felt she knew this Geoffrey very well. He described his country life, talking about the people in the nearby village, about his occasional clashes with the vicar, and that he planned to go up to London soon.

In the last e-mail, he suggested they meet in London for dinner.

Agatha agreed. To her surprise, he suggested that restaurant in Chinatown where she had met her previous date. Agatha said she would prefer somewhere else.

Three days passed without a reply. Agatha could hardly concentrate on her work. Then finally an e-mail arrived suggesting a rendezvous at a restaurant called The Lifeboat in Saint Katherine's Dock at eight o'clock on Saturday evening.

Agatha cheerfully e-mailed an acceptance and phoned Mrs. Bloxby with the good news. She then made appointments with the beautician and hairdresser for Saturday morning.

Mrs. Bloxby was sitting in a dentist's waiting room on Saturday afternoon. A filling had fallen out of a tooth. She felt she was lucky to get an appointment because most dentists shut down for the weekend. It was a private dentist and Mrs. Bloxby hoped the treatment would not turn out to be too expensive. The woman who had gone in before her seemed to have been in the treatment room for ages. Mrs. Bloxby wished she had brought a book.

Mrs. Bloxby flicked through the pages of a copy of *Country Life*. She wished there were still magazines around with stories in them. She remembered when magazines like *Good Housekeeping* would serialize authors like Ruth Rendell.

And then she flicked it open at a double-page spread of photographs. Mrs. Bloxby could hardly believe her eyes. It was a feature on the recent wedding of Geoffrey Camden. With shaking hands, she took out her mobile and asked directory enquiries for the number of Geoffrey Camden at The Grange in Shropshire. When she got the number, she asked to be connected. A woman answered the phone. Mrs. Bloxby asked to speak to Mr. Camden.

"This is Mrs. Camden," said the woman. "Geoffrey's up in London to see an old friend. He won't be back until tomorrow."

Agatha must be warned. Mrs. Bloxby dialled Agatha's mobile. It was switched off.

Then she wondered if Geoffrey Camden, so recently married, would be the type of man to cheat on his wife—through a dating agency, of all things.

And fast on that came one dreadful thought—Sylvan.

What if Sylvan were tricking Agatha? Desperately she phoned Toni and explained the situation. Toni said she would phone Bill Wong and get up to London herself. Bill listened carefully but said he could hardly alert Scotland Yard on such a far-fetched theory. With the whole of Interpol still looking for Sylvan, he would hardly dare put in an appearance, but he would go up to London with Toni.

On the road to London, Toni phoned James and Charles and then phoned Roy Silver. But Roy was out. She left a message for him telling him to get down to Saint Katherine's Dock and warn Agatha.

Agatha was ten minutes early when she arrived at the restaurant. The restaurant was very dark. Behind her a waiter asked her if she would like something to drink. Agatha ordered a Campari and soda. When it arrived, she sipped it as she studied the menu. It was one of those twee menus she hated so much: the Captain's Table Special for two, Dirty Dick's shrimp cocktail, Captain Hook's battered cod and so on.

She began to feel slightly dizzy. She pulled out her mobile phone and switched it on in case he was going to be late and had been trying to contact her.

Toni's voice came on the phone. "Get out of there, Agatha. It's a trick. It could be Sylvan."

Agatha stumbled to her feet, staggered and almost fell. A smooth French voice said, "I'm afraid the lady has had too much to drink. I'll help her outside."

Agatha opened her mouth to scream but the restaurant swirled around her and something seemed to have happened to her voice. It was like one of those nightmares where you tried to scream and only whimpering little squeaks came out.

She had only taken a sip of the Campari and soda,

thinking it a sophisticated drink, although it was one she did not like very much.

The air outside revived her and she began to struggle weakly. "There is a gun in your ribs," said Sylvan. "One squawk out of you and you're dead."

Bill, followed by Toni, rushed into the restaurant. The first thing Toni's eyes spotted was Agatha's handbag resting on a chair. "Where is the lady who belongs to this?" she shouted. The manager came forward. "The lady had a dizzy turn and one of our waiters took her outside for some fresh air."

"Was he French?"

"Yes, he was filling in for one of our waiters who was taken ill suddenly."

Bill took out his phone and called Scotland Yard while Toni rushed out to the dock. Saint Katherine's Dock is punnily named The Berth of London. Cruisers and yachts bobbed at anchor. Toni went up to an old man who was watching the boats.

"Did a boat just leave here?" she asked.

"Yes," he said. "She was a big powerful motor cruiser."

"Name."

"What?"

"The name of the boat?" shouted Toni.

"*Versales.*"

"Versailles?"

"Could be. Never could get my tongue round them French names."

Bill came to join her. "The River Police will be with us in a minute. We've got to catch him before he throws her overboard."

Agatha stared bleakly at Sylvan, who was sitting across from her in the boat's cabin. "I see your old friend, Jerry Carton, is driving us. What are you going to do with me?"

"Get you out to sea and chuck you overboard. The water's nice and cold this time of year."

"But they'll know it was you."

He gave a Gallic shrug. "They haven't caught me yet."

"Why? Why do you want to kill me?"

"Revenge, pure and simple. To think I even encouraged Olivia to hire you? I thought that would make me look innocent, but then I realized your poking about was becoming a threat. You fouled up my nice lucrative business."

"But why shoot Felicity?"

"Ah, I did not do that. That was George."

"Her own father!"

"Remember, he wasn't her father. He'd been having sex with her since she was fourteen. She promised him that they could carry on after she was married. She was, after all, sex-obsessed. But the wedding went to her head. She told him she wouldn't have anything to do with him after the wedding. He tried to force her. She said she was going to tell Olivia, her mother, everything. So he put on—how you call it?—a boiler suit, gloves, plastic boots, the lot, and shot her through the window to make it look as if some outsider had done it. He shoved the boiler suit and everything in the furnace."

"And the gun?" asked Agatha.

"Ah, the local police of course never thought to search any of us. George simply pushed it into the waistband of his trousers under his morning coat, called the police, followed them to the church and slipped it to me."

"And what did you do with it?"

"Threw it in the river at the first opportunity."

"Where in the river?"

"There is no point in telling you because you are not going to escape me this time."

Desperate to keep him talking, Agatha asked, "Why did you kill George?"

"He'd become dangerously sentimental, mourning Felicity, and he was beginning to drink too much. Hélas, he had to go."

"How did you get my details from the agency?"

"Easy. The joke is I hired a detective agency to follow you. I found out about the bankrupt agency and saw the fair Amanda and said I would put in a bid if I could take over her client list. She jumped at it. She expects me to be at her lawyer's tomorrow. She will be disappointed."

"Why did you kill Sean?"

"The idiot had the nerve to blackmail me. He said I wasn't paying him enough for helping smuggle those Chinese into the country."

"And what about poor Bert?"

"That one was always crawling about in the dark. He saw me unloading a cargo. He tried to blackmail me. Silly boy must have hoped to get money out of you as well. Two blackmailers. Pouf! Both dead."

"You are one nasty bastard," said Agatha. "You are lower than whale shit."

"But you, chérie, are nearly dead, so why not shut up and say your prayers. You're about to go to sleep anyway."

Keeping the gun on her, with his other hand he opened a box and took out a syringe. "Don't want you swimming around getting help from any passing boat," said Sylvan.

"Why don't you just shoot me?"

"In this tiny space, the bullet might either ricochet or make a hole in my nice new boat." The table was between them. Agatha made a lunge for the gun, but he snatched it before she could get to it. He struck her on the side of the head with the butt and Agatha slumped back.

"Why didn't I think of that before?" he muttered. "Now you are nice and quiet."

Through a red haze, Agatha watched him fill the syringe. Then, with all her remaining strength, she dived across the table and seized the syringe and plunged it into his neck. He scrabbled for the gun and then fired just as Agatha fell under the table.

There was a long silence. Agatha eased herself up. Jerry, she thought. I've got to deal with Jerry. Sylvan was out cold.

Holding the gun, Agatha dragged herself upstairs. She rammed the muzzle into Jerry's neck and said, "Turn the boat around."

He drove his elbow into her stomach and she went flying backwards and the gun flew out of her grasp and skittered across the cockpit.

Jerry cut the engine and turned round with a gun in his hand. Just as the shot went off, Agatha forced herself backwards and fell down the companionway.

She shut her eyes, bruised and battered, thinking that she could no longer escape death.

A stentorian voice shouted, "Police!" and floodlight shone in the cabin windows.

Agatha hunched herself into the fetal position. She heard a splash and a voice shouting, "Get him. He's in the water."

Then she heard feet above her landing on the deck. The first policeman came clattering down the steps. "Mrs. Raisin? Are you Mrs. Agatha Raisin?"

Agatha croaked, "Yes."

More men came down and helped her up. "That's Sylvan Dubois," said Agatha, swaying in their arms. "I stabbed him with his own hypodermic."

"Let's get you to hospital. That's a nasty bash on the head," said one.

For the first time since Sylvan had struck her, Agatha became aware of blood running down the side of her head.

She was helped tenderly onto the nearest police launch. There were three, and in one of them she could see Jerry being dragged out of the water and handcuffed.

"It's over at last," said Agatha, and burying her face in the chest of the nearest policeman, she burst into tears.

Agatha was welcomed at Saint Katherine's Dock by Toni, Bill, Charles, James and Roy. James hugged her and Toni demanded to know if they'd got Sylvan.

An inspector with the River Police said sternly, "Mrs. Raisin will need to be taken to hospital. Leave your questions until later." Agatha was helped into a waiting ambulance.

"Here comes Sylvan," shouted Toni. "Is he dead?"

Agatha turned round, one foot on the step of the ambulance. "Just drugged. I stabbed him with his own syringe."

Chapter Ten

AGATHA WAS SEDATED after her head had been examined. She was told she had received a nasty blow and was slightly concussed but otherwise she was all right.

She awoke the next day to find two Special Branch detectives beside her bed. She was questioned for an hour until a doctor interrupted and said that she needed more rest.

It was to be the beginning of days of questioning. Toni arrived with a present of a bottle of French perfume. Then there was James bearing chocolates and Charles with nothing, although he ate half the box of chocolates. Roy came in carrying a palm tree in a pot, deaf to the shouts of the nurses that no flowers were allowed. "It's not flowers," complained Roy sulkily. "It's a tree." But the palm was taken away from him and he was told he could collect it on his way out.

Then the reassuring presence of Mrs. Bloxby arrived. She had got Doris Simpson to search Agatha's bedroom for the prettiest nightdress and the bathroom for a supply of make-up along with a suitcase of her clothes. Agatha listened as she heard for the first time how Mrs. Bloxby had found out that her date was a fake by seeing Geoffrey Camden's marriage in the pages of *Country Life*.

"I'm surprised the press have not been to see me," said Agatha.

"Oh, they're all camped outside."

"Is Toni still around? She was here this morning."

"She is very fond of you. I believe she is staying in London and plans to run you home."

Agatha scowled. "Has she said anything to the press?"

"She just says 'No comment,' like the rest of us."

Agatha picked up the phone beside her bed and dialled Toni's number. "Toni, dear," Mrs. Bloxby heard Agatha say, "there's no need to hang around for me. Could you get back to the office and make sure things are running smoothly? No, it's all right. James will be running me back."

"And is he?" asked Mrs. Bloxby when Agatha had rung off.

"Yes, I think so," said Agatha.

Mrs. Bloxby repressed a smile. Agatha wanted her moment of glory with the press and without pretty Toni around to take away the limelight.

"Actually, I drove up," said Mrs. Bloxby. "Did you come by car?"

"No, I came by train. My car's at the station in Moreton. I feel fighting fit. I wonder if they'd let me leave today."

"You could ask and I could drive you home."

"That would be great. I think the police have winkled every bit of information out of me they can."

The doctor was summoned and said that provided she was not going to drive herself, she was free to go.

Agatha retreated to the bathroom with the suitcase of clothes and make-up bag and changed. She washed, dried her hair and brushed it until it shone. The perks of being a heroine were that she had a private hospital room and a bathroom all to herself.

Mrs. Bloxby tactfully hung back as Agatha emerged from the hospital to face a battery of press and television. Mindful of police warnings not to say anything that might jeopardize the trial, she made a short statement and then posed for pictures. Something was jabbing at her conscience and she suddenly realized what it was. If it hadn't been for Mrs. Bloxby, then she, Agatha, would surely be dead.

But if she brought Mrs. Bloxby forward to the press,

they would learn that she had been trying to find a man through a dating agency.

It would all come out in court, but Agatha meanly decided it could wait until then.

Agatha was worried about her age. She felt she was becoming more fragile. It seemed to take a long time to get over the shock of her near death. Mrs. Bloxby suggested counselling, Bill Wong suggested victim support, but Agatha did not want to talk to any therapist or psychiatrist about her inner thoughts, mostly because half the time she did not know what they were anyway, and found life easier if she just ploughed on.

The weather was dismal. Heavy rain causing flooding and the river Avon in Evesham was rising dangerously again. But mostly there was plenty of work to keep her occupied. Quite often she worked late, not wanting to go back to her empty cottage, until she remembered her cats and dragged herself off home.

She spent Christmas at Bill's home, even though the dinner was foul and his parents seemed to dislike her as much as ever—although Agatha comforted herself with the thought that they didn't really seem to like anyone apart from their adored son.

January brought in some brisk, clear, sunny, frosty days

and Agatha regained her spirits and self-confidence and began to feel like her old self again.

By the end of January, she found a new friend. She had taken time off from work to look round the market in Mircester, buying up local produce and meat, determined to eat healthily, trying to shove to the back of her mind that she would end up as usual putting something in the microwave and giving what she had bought to Doris Simpson. She was standing at the fruit and vegetable stall when a woman next to her dropped her shopping bag and carrots and onions rolled out onto the street. Agatha helped her pick them up.

"Thanks," said the woman. "I really am clumsy."

"That's all right," said Agatha with a rare burst of honesty. "I'm pretty clumsy myself."

She studied Agatha's face. "Haven't I seen you somewhere before?"

"My photo's been in the newspapers," said Agatha proudly.

"I know! You're that famous detective! Agatha Raisin."

"That's me."

"Look. I've just moved into the area. Can I buy you lunch?"

Agatha studied her. She was possibly in her forties with expensively blonded hair, a smooth, lightly tanned face and wearing a mink coat. Wearing a mink coat in broad daylight took courage in these days of political correctness. There was a heavy gold necklace at her throat and a Rolex on her wrist.

"All right," said Agatha. "But I can't be away from the office too long."

Over lunch in The George hotel, the woman introduced herself as Charlotte Rother. She listened, fascinated, as Agatha recounted her adventures. By the time the coffee arrived, Agatha realized guiltily that she hadn't asked her new companion about herself.

"There's not much to tell," said Charlotte. "I'm a divorcee. My husband was very, very rich and gave me a handsome settlement. Fortunately, we don't have any children. I was living in London, but I'm tired of cities. I've bought a cottage in Ancombe. Do you know it?"

"Yes," said Agatha. "It's quite near me. I live in Carsely."

"Do you have one of those thatched cottages?"

"Yes."

"So pretty, but surely very expensive to maintain."

"Thatching does cost a lot. What type of place do you have?"

"It's a bungalow. Not very attractive. But the area is pretty and I have a good garden. Are you interested in gardening?"

"I really don't have the time. I get a man round to keep what's there tidy."

Charlotte had a singularly warm and charming smile. "Why don't you come and visit me this weekend and I'll show you the place."

Agatha thought of the empty weekend looming up and said cheerfully, "I'd love to."

"Come for lunch. About one. Do you know where the church is in Ancombe?"

"Yes, right in the middle."

"As you drive past, coming from Carsely, count along six houses after the church and I am the seventh on the left. It's got a short drive and it's bordered by a high hedge, so don't miss it."

"I won't." Agatha smiled. "And as I am going to lunch at your place, I insist on paying for this lunch. No. No arguments."

They exchanged cards and when she went back to the office, Agatha felt pleased with her new friend. Of course, Mrs. Bloxby was really her best friend, but the vicar's wife was often busy and had too many parish commitments to go out for meals or to the theatre.

She did not talk to anyone about Charlotte. She wanted to keep her to herself.

So Agatha was really annoyed when her doorbell rang on Saturday morning to find Roy Silver on her doorstep, complete with overnight bag.

"Roy! I'm usually glad to see you," said Agatha, "but I've got an important lunch date. You should have phoned."

"I'm sorry. I'm having a horrible time." Tears began to run down Roy's face.

"Oh, come in, do. Tell me what's been happening."

Roy followed her into the kitchen. "I got an offer from another PR agency."

"Which one?"

"Atherton's."

"They're very big."

"I was so excited," said Roy, mopping his eyes. "I went round to see them as arranged. I was interviewed by Bertha Atherton."

"Snakes and bastards. She's a complete cow."

"So it turns out. I had just got handed the Duluxe makeup launch. Bertha offered me a lot of money. I said I'd join them."

"Let me guess," said Agatha. "She then went straight to Duluxe and said she was hiring their PR so it would be better all round if they moved the account to her."

"That's it. Duluxe told Pedman's and Mr. Pedman called me in and gave me such a bawling-out."

"Did he fire you?"

"No, I swore blind that Atherton's had called me round for an interview and had offered me a lot of money and all I said was that I would think about it. I mean, I didn't sign anything. I don't think she recorded anything. There was to be a further meeting next week."

"During which time," said Agatha, "Bertha would find

out whether she could winkle the account away from Pedman's, and if she couldn't she'd simply have phoned you up and said she'd changed her mind."

"That's it. Everyone in the office is treating me like a leper. And there's a new PR snapping at my heels and trying to take the account away from me."

"Has Pedman shown any sign of doing that?"

"No."

"Then he won't. Do a good job with Duluxe." Agatha bit her lip. She had been accused before of having a cavalier attitude towards her old friends.

"Unpack your bag and leave me to phone," she said.

As soon as Roy had trailed upstairs to the spare bedroom to unpack, Agatha found Charlotte's card and phoned her.

"Don't worry," said Charlotte gaily. "Bring your friend along. There's masses to eat."

"Now, I want you to be charming," lectured Agatha as she drove Roy to Ancombe.

"I'm always charming," said Roy sulkily.

"Right. Here's the church. Now I've got to count the houses. Right, here we are. Yes, she does have a big hedge. If she wants to garden, she'll need to cut that down a bit. It must cut off light from half the garden."

The inside of Charlotte's sitting room came as something of a shock. Agatha thought that someone with such impeccable dress sense as Charlotte would have had something classier in the way of furnishings. There was an oatmeal-coloured three-piece suite in front of a glass coffee table. A rather noisy flowery wallpaper covered the walls. Beside the sofa was one of those cheap nests of tables one got in DIY shops. The curtains at the windows were of the awful frilly scalloped kind looking like so many knicker-covered backsides. The fire was a two-bar electric one with fake logs.

"Awful, isn't it?" said Charlotte. "I bought the whole place, furniture and all. I'll be getting rid of this lot soon."

Agatha introduced Roy. Over pre-lunch drinks, Roy poured out his tale of woe, much to Agatha's annoyance, but Charlotte was sympathetic. Agatha revealed that she used to work in public relations herself and both women then set about cheering Roy up by suggesting outrageous ways in which he could promote Duluxe.

Lunch was delicious. Smoked salmon was followed by roast pheasant with roast parsnips and roast potatoes and broccoli. Dessert was that Cotswold favourite—icky-sticky pudding.

Agatha could feel the waistband of her skirt tightening and envied Charlotte her slim figure.

When she and Roy were leaving, Agatha suggested that

she and Charlotte should meet up during the week, but Charlotte said she had to go to London but would phone Agatha immediately she got back.

Before Roy left, Agatha had drafted out a whole series of proposals for the launch of Duluxe. As soon as he got to the office on Monday morning, Roy sent the proposals into Mr. Pedman, without mentioning Agatha's name, and found himself back in favour again. He was told that Sarah Andrews, director of Duluxe, wished to take him out to dinner that evening at the Ivy restaurant.

Roy met her clutching a spare set of Agatha's proposals, by which time he had convinced himself they had all been his own idea. But he had phoned Agatha before he left for dinner to thank her. She warned him severely to dress conservatively.

At the Ivy, Roy basked in the praise of Sarah Andrews. He was in a part of the restaurant which was cut off from the main room by a glass-and-wood screen. A couple on the other side were chattering in rapid French. When Sarah left to go to the toilet, Roy, always on the lookout for celebrities, peered round the screen and then drew back. The couple speaking in rapid French were Charlotte and some man.

He returned to his chair, his mind working furiously. Agatha and Charlotte had told him how they had met.

When Sarah returned, she teased him about seeming abstracted and Roy said he couldn't stop thinking up new ideas for Duluxe.

Roy returned to his flat after dinner feeling worried. He should have spoken to Charlotte. He wondered if Agatha was being set up by a friend of Sylvan's. It seemed very far-fetched.

He phoned Agatha, who listened to him carefully and then said, "But you don't speak French."

"I know a few words," said Roy huffily. "And she was rattling along like a native."

"Why didn't you speak to her?"

"I got worried. I thought Sylvan might have got someone on the outside to get to you."

"Rubbish! Oh, well, I'll do some research. I've got a week."

Agatha went to her computer, switched it on, and Googled Charlotte Rother, not really expecting anything to come up. To her surprise, there were three news stories featured. She opened one. Charlotte Rother had made the papers when she had obtained a divorce settlement of five million pounds from her entrepreneur husband, John Rother. There was a photograph of her leaving court. She had put a hand up to shield her face, but the blonde hair, the clothes and the mink coat worn open were all the same as her Charlotte's.

Agatha tried the other two stories. All pretty much the same, but one had a clear photo of Charlotte. She looked strained and had obviously been crying, but it was the Charlotte Agatha knew. She phoned Roy back in triumph.

"Now I feel silly," he said. "But be careful all the same."

But Roy somehow couldn't let the matter go. He phoned Toni and suggested it would do no harm if one of them could check up on this woman without letting Agatha know.

Toni knew that as her photograph and Sharon's had been in the newspapers, she'd better see if someone else at the agency might like to find out a few things.

Early next morning, she called on Phil Marshall. He listened to her carefully and then said, "But Agatha seems to have checked her out very well. I mean, what if she does speak French? Lots of rich cosmopolitan people do. Oh, well. I'll tell Agatha I want a few days off and I'll see what I can dig up."

Phil went first to the offices of the *Cotswolds Journal* and painstakingly began to read through the property advertisements in the back numbers. At last, after almost a whole day of searching, he found an advertisement for the bungalow in Ancombe.

He went to the estate agent's and asked when the sale had gone through. "Just three weeks ago," said the agent. "With the market being so bad, we thought we would never shift it. In fact, it's difficult to sell anything. Mrs. Rother paid the asking price provided the furnishings were thrown in as well. It belonged to a middle-aged lady who died last year and her daughter lives abroad and didn't want the job of clearing the house and asked us if we could find a buyer who would take everything."

"Did she pay by cheque?" asked Phil.

"Of course."

That seemed to be that. He phoned Toni.

But somehow, a nagging doubt would not leave Toni. Identities could be pinched. She Googled the divorce case and took a note of Mr. John Rother's office address. She phoned, and reverting to her original Gloucestershire accent, which she had "poshed up" after working for Agatha, said that she had been cleaning for Mrs. Rother, who wanted her services again but she did not have an address for her.

Toni was lucky in that Mr. Rother's secretary loathed the ex-Mrs. Rother and saw no need to protect her address. "It's fifty-one Alexandria Mews, Kensington," she said.

Toni found the telephone number was ex-directory and resolved to go up to town the following Saturday. Why should Charlotte Rother still have the London address and yet want some undistinguished bungalow in Ancombe?

Agatha had invited Charlotte around to her cottage for lunch on Saturday. Charlotte made flattering comments on the beauty of the old cottage. But she ignored Agatha's cats and they ignored her in turn. Agatha felt obscurely like a mother whose children have been insulted and then chided herself for being weird.

They had a pleasant lunch. Charlotte complimented Agatha on her cooking and Agatha hoped that the empty packets of Marks & Spencer meals were carefully hidden.

After lunch, Charlotte said, "It's a lovely day. I've always wanted to see Warwick Castle."

"It's not far," said Agatha. "I'll drive you."

"No, I'll drive. After all your hard work preparing lunch, it's the least I can do."

Agatha's phone rang just as they were leaving. It was Toni. "I wondered how you were getting on," said Toni. "Fine," replied Agatha. "Can't speak. Just off to Warwick Castle."

Toni found the address in Alexandria Mews and rang the bell. There was no reply. Well, that figures, thought Toni. If she is who she says she is, then she'll be down in the Cotswolds.

But she knelt down and looked through the letter box. A sports car roared past behind her. Then there was relative silence. Toni thought she could hear something. She pressed her ear to the letter box. There were faint sounds like, "Mmmph. Mmmph."

Toni thought quickly. She took out her mobile and called the police and waited anxiously until ten minutes later, and with agonizing slowness, a police car cruised into the mews.

A large beefy police sergeant got out. "What is all this then about someone trapped inside?"

"I can hear sounds from inside but she doesn't answer the door," said Toni. "Put your ear to the letter box."

He bent down. His colleague stood behind him, grinning.

Then the sergeant straightened up. "Can't hear a thing."

"But I heard something," pleaded Toni.

"Like what?"

"Sort of muffled, strangled noises."

The sergeant rang the bell. A neighbour came out of the next mews cottage and stared at them curiously. "What's the person's name?" asked the sergeant.

"Mrs. Charlotte Rother."

"That's that woman who was divorced recently," said his colleague.

The neighbour came up to them. "What's going on?"

"This little lady," said the sergeant, "thinks she can hear sinister noises from inside. Have you seen Mrs. Rother lately?"

"Not for a couple of weeks or something like that."

"There's a pane of glass on the door," said Toni. "You could smash that and maybe get in."

"Here now, Miss . . ."

"Toni Gilmour."

"Miss Gilmour. We don't go around breaking into property just like that. What's your business with her?"

"I'm a private detective and I think someone may have stolen her identity."

"And why would she do that?"

Fighting for patience, Toni explained about Sylvan Dubois and how he may have sent an impostor after Agatha.

The sergeant said heavily, "We'll go back to the station and make some phone calls."

"But it may be too late!"

He gave her a cynical look, nodded to his colleague and both got back in the car and drove off. The neighbour went back indoors.

Toni looked up and down the quiet mews. No one was about. She saw a brick lying some distance away. She went and picked it up and smashed the pane of glass on the door, reached inside and turned the handle. There was nothing in the small downstairs living room. She ran upstairs. There was a kitchen on the landing area with a corridor leading off it.

Toni thrust open the door of a bedroom. Handcuffed to the bed lay a woman with a gag over her mouth. Toni ripped off the gag and felt for a pulse on the woman's neck. The pulse was faint but she was alive.

Toni called the police and asked for an ambulance. Then she phoned Agatha. There was no reply, not even from an operator to say the phone was switched off. Charles lived in Warwickshire. Toni phoned him and got past his manservant by screaming it was a matter of life and death. Charles listened and said, "Warwick Castle? I'm on my way. I'll phone the police on the road there."

Agatha had been to Warwick Castle before. Charlotte exclaimed over the beauty of the medieval building. They visited the battlements, the towers and the torture chamber, Madame Tussaud's waxworks inside, and then Charlotte said, "I'm exhausted. I could do with a cup of tea."

"And I could do with going to the loo," said Agatha. "I'll join you in the tea room."

"Want any cakes or buns?"

"No, just tea," said Agatha.

In the toilet, Agatha fought down a feeling of uneasiness about Charlotte. In the castle drawing room, when she had been looking at a picture, she had seen a reflection of Charlotte's face in the dark glass-framed portrait. Charlotte's face seemed to be distorted by a look of malice. I'm imagining things, thought Agatha. But no one knows where I am. I'll just make a few phone calls. Agatha had left her BlackBerry at home and was carrying her old mobile phone with her. Sometimes she felt more at ease with a simple phone and took it on local trips in case her car broke down.

In the toilet, she checked her phone for messages and found it was totally dead. She scowled down at it. She had charged it up the night before.

Agatha suddenly had a memory of walking down the garden with her cats before she left and when she had walked back up, Charlotte was bent over the kitchen table and Agatha's bag was open and Agatha could now not remember leaving her bag open.

She opened up the back of her phone and searched for the SIM card. It had been taken out.

Agatha found her hands were beginning to shake. She used the toilet and washed her hands, wondering what to do. Why should Charlotte disable her phone? So that you can't call for help, you gullible idiot, sneered a voice in her brain.

Why Warwick Castle? Maybe Charlotte planned to take her on a walk round the rose garden, say, plunge a hypodermic into her in a quiet corner and leave her to rot.

Sylvan, thought Agatha bitterly. His long arm had reached out from the prison. She pinned a smile on her face and returned to the table.

"I nearly came to look for you," said Charlotte. "You were ages."

Agatha noticed Charlotte had a small clutch handbag whereas her own was a large leather one.

"Goodness, look at that!" shrieked Agatha suddenly. "Over there!"

"What? Where?"

"Stand up and have a look out of the window."

When Charlotte got to her feet, Agatha deftly slid Charlotte's little handbag across the table and dropped it into her own. Then she emptied her cup of tea back into the pot in case Charlotte had put something into it.

"I can't see anything," said Charlotte, coming back to the table. "What was it?"

"A peacock."

"Agatha, the place is full of peacocks."

"I still get excited when I see one," said Agatha.

"Where's my bag?" said Charlotte.

"I don't know. Did you have it when we came into the restaurant?"

"I'm sure I did."

"Charles!" cried Agatha, feeling she could have wept with relief as his familiar figure walked into the tea room.

"Hi, Agatha," said Charles. "Do you know the place is swarming with police? I wonder what's going on."

Charlotte rose unsteadily to her feet. "Just going to get some air," she said.

Agatha made a grab for her but she twisted away and ran for the door. Agatha followed, shouting to the nearest policeman, "That's her!"

"Hold back, Agatha," said Charles quietly. "It's up to the police now."

Charlotte zigzagged across the lawn and then dived into the entrance to the battlements. Charles and Agatha walked outside the tea room and watched the chase.

Charlotte appeared, a tiny figure up on the battlements, rushing this way and that, but her escape was now blocked by the police.

Her last cry was faintly borne to their ears as she threw herself off.

People rushed forwards and then were herded away by the police. "Let's not look," said Charles. "Let's just go and sit down in the tea room."

"How did you know?" asked Agatha.

Charles told her about the phone call from Toni and about how Toni had found the real Mrs. Rother.

"I knew there was something up when my phone didn't work," said Agatha. "She'd disabled it. I pinched her handbag in case she had something nasty in there for me."

"Let's have a look."

The tea room was empty, everyone having rushed outside to see what was happening.

Agatha took out the small clutch handbag and opened it. "Don't touch anything," said Charles. "Just look."

"There's a syringe in here," said Agatha. "Why didn't she just bump me off at home? Why Warwick Castle?"

"She must have wanted you really off guard and surrounded by crowds of tourists."

Two plain-clothes detectives came in. "Mrs. Raisin?"

"Yes."

"Will you come with us? We have a lot of questions to ask you."

Agatha was interviewed at police headquarters in Leamington Spa for a long time. Then she was taken to Mircester headquarters, where the questioning started all over again.

Wilkes asked her at one point why she had not suspected Charlotte earlier. Agatha said she had no reason to. She had thought that there might be a remote chance that Sylvan would send someone after her, but she had thought that person would be a man. And all the time during the questioning, Agatha's spirits sank lower and lower. Had it not been for discovering her phone had been tampered with, had it not been for Toni's and Roy's suspicions, then she might have been killed.

The police made her feel like a bumbling amateur, and by the time she was released and returned wearily to her cottage, that is exactly how she felt.

There were only two local reporters waiting on her doorstep to interview her. Agatha rallied enough to give them a few brief quotes but wondered where the national press and television were. She was to find out next day that they had decided to go with the better story.

Toni's face was all over the front pages. The real Charlotte Rother, photographed in hospital, was hailing her as the heroine who had saved her life. She said that the woman who had stolen her identity had drugged her and tied her to the bed. Her real name turned out to be Clarice Delavalle, one of Sylvan's former mistresses, who bore a remarkable resemblance to Charlotte. Clarice had returned from time to time to feed her and then had not come back and Charlotte was suddenly sure she meant to leave her to starve to death. Also, Clarice had taken her fur coat and jewellery.

Roy Silver had also been interviewed, saying he had seen and heard Clarice in the Ivy talking in French, and had urged Toni to check up on her. The Warwick Castle adventure was reported on the inside pages. There was a head and shoulders photograph of Agatha taken some time ago, scowling at the camera. Reports of the fake Charlotte's suicide had been taken from eyewitnesses amongst the tourists.

Like all people who don't really quite know who they are and consider their job their identity, Agatha felt totally diminished.

She went up to her bedroom, undressed and showered and then crept under the duvet.

She fell down into a dream where she was trying to get into the office in the morning but her keys would not work. She phoned Toni, who said they had all decided for the health of the agency it would be better if she retired.

Chapter Eleven

AGATHA WAS AWAKENED by the harsh ringing of the phone beside the bed. It was Mrs. Bloxby. "Are you all right, Mrs. Raisin?" came her anxious voice. "I have called at your cottage several times but you did not answer the door."

"I'm in bed," said Agatha. "I'll be round to see you as soon as I get dressed."

"Actually, I'm outside."

"I'll be right down."

When Agatha opened the door, Mrs. Bloxby looked at her worriedly. Agatha had not removed her make-up before going to bed and melting mascara had left black rings under her eyes.

"Come into the kitchen," said Agatha. "I need a black coffee and a cigarette."

Before sitting down at the kitchen table, Agatha switched on a recently installed extractor fan in the window before lighting a cigarette.

Mrs. Bloxby watched her friend sucking smoke down into her lungs and said anxiously, "Don't you ever worry about lung cancer?"

"From time to time. I'll stop next month."

"Why next month?"

"Because I need a holiday. Toni can run things," added Agatha bitterly.

Mrs. Bloxby saw the newspapers spread out on the table. "You must be very grateful to Miss Gilmour," said the vicar's wife.

"I should be, I know. But she's made me feel like a rank amateur."

"Think of all the cases you've solved."

Agatha took a gulp of black coffee. "So what? That was then. This is now."

"You have had several bad frights and yet you refuse to go for counselling. You should get some help."

"I'm all right," said Agatha. "I need to get away and think. I might give up the agency altogether."

Mrs. Bloxby looked appalled. "And put all your staff out of work in the middle of a recession!"

"Well, maybe that is a bit extreme. I'll be all right when I get away for a break."

"Have you ever heard about taking yourself with you? You can't get rid of your problems by running away."

"Spare me the psychobabble."

Mrs. Bloxby gathered up her handbag and stood up. "I'm off. Call me if you need me."

Agatha was appalled when she realized she had been rude to her best friend. Then she thought, oh, what does it all matter? Nobody needs me. I must get away.

Two weeks later, Agatha sat in a café opposite the Blue Mosque in Istanbul feeling like a new woman. She had been to beauty salons, hairdressers and masseurs. Her hip had not ached once. The weather was sunny and mild. She had plenty of books to read and was in the grip of Eric Ambler's *Journey Into Fear.*

Her jealousy of Toni, her shocks at the attempts on her life seemed to have sailed away down the Bosphorus. At one point, she glanced up from her book and became aware that a man at a table opposite was watching her. He was tall with hooded eyes, a beaky nose and a firm mouth. He had thick brown hair, beautifully cut, although his dark suit looked worn.

He smiled, and for some reason Agatha found herself smiling back. He rose and came to join her. "American?" he asked.

"No, English," said Agatha. "Are you a tourist?"

"No, I live in Istanbul."

"Your English is excellent."

"Thank you. Is that a very good book?"

"Excellent."

"Then I'll leave you in peace to read it."

To Agatha's surprise, he did not go away, but sat down again. He lit a cigarette, leaned back in his chair and surveyed the passing crowds.

The muezzins began the call to prayer.

Agatha stopped reading. She was suddenly hungry. She picked up the menu on the table.

"I'll take you to lunch," said her companion.

"Why?"

"You interest me."

"Is this a pickup?" demanded Agatha.

"Meaning what?"

"Are you trying to get off with me?"

"I don't understand that either. Would I like to get to know you better? Yes. Just lunch."

"Oh, all right," said Agatha.

They walked across the square, over the tramlines and into a dark cellar-type restaurant.

"You'd better order," said Agatha. "My knowledge of Turkish food is pretty much limited to kebab."

The meal was delicious, starting with a cheese pastry as light as a feather followed by lamb cooked slowly in the oven with raisins. Outside, the sunlit crowd flowed up and down.

He had asked Agatha what she did and her descriptions of her detective prowess took up much of the meal. And as she talked, she could feel her old confidence in her abilities returning.

She refused a dessert and settled for coffee instead but decided against drinking brandy because she had already drunk quite a lot of wine.

"What do you do?" she asked.

"I'm a civil servant. I work for the government."

"Which branch?"

"The tax office."

"And are you usually allowed such a lot of time off work?"

"I'm taking a few days' leave."

"Are you married?" asked Agatha bluntly.

"Was. Got divorced five years ago. You?"

"Divorced as well. What is your name?"

"Mustafa Kemal. And you?"

"Agatha Raisin."

"That's a funny name."

"What's funny about it?"

"Raisin. Those wrinkly dried grapes. No, don't scowl. A pretty woman like you should not scowl."

"Tell me about the tax office," said Agatha.

"There's not much to tell. It is very boring."

"Did you ever think of getting another job?"

"Not really. My family were so proud of me. My mother was a dressmaker and my father, a labourer. I was the first to go to university. Now I am too old to change."

"How old are you?"

"Fifty-four."

"That's not too old to change!"

"Agatha, as far as jobs are concerned, it's too old anywhere."

After lunch he escorted her to her hotel and asked her if she would like to have dinner with him that evening. Agatha happily agreed.

She spent the rest of the day wrapped in rosy dreams of being married in Istanbul. No more detective work. No more feelings of failure. Mustafa obviously thought her a very attractive woman. She felt young again, full of anticipation.

And when he saw her in the foyer of the hotel wearing a black dress, slit up one side to reveal one shapely leg and his eyes lit up with admiration, Agatha glowed.

He drove her up to the old fire tower which dominates the skyline of Istanbul. On the road there, Agatha, looking out of the car window, saw Erol Fehim, the man who had helped her before.

"Stop the car," she shouted. "I think I've seen someone I know."

But he did not seem to hear her and drove on. When they reached the fire tower, they climbed the stairs to the restaurant. They had a table by the window. The view was stunning. Down below, a fountain sparkled in the Golden Horn and there was a magnificent panorama of the palaces and minarets of the great city.

Dinner included a floor show of mainly traditional Turkish acts. The show started with a too-thin belly dancer whose act seemed to go on forever. Then there was a Black Sea troupe who balanced knives on their noses and threw them at a target. It was very loud and noisy and conversation was limited.

Agatha excused herself and went in search of the toilets. She had a sudden desire to share the news that she was in love. She was so sure she was in love.

She phoned Mrs. Bloxby and told her the news. "When did you meet him?" asked the vicar's wife.

"Just today."

"Mrs. Raisin!"

"No, this is the real thing."

"What's his name?"

"Mustafa Kemal."

There was a little silence and then Mrs. Bloxby said, "That's odd."

"What's odd?"

"Mustafa Kemal was the name of Ataturk, the founder of modern Turkey. Are you sure it isn't another of Sylvan Dubois's associates?"

Agatha felt suddenly cold. "I'll call you back." She thought about how easily she had been picked up. She clung on to the handbasin, feeling dizzy. Then she straightened up and squared her shoulders. She accosted the first waiter at the entrance to the restaurant and hissed, "Call the police."

He looked at her, puzzled, and then signalled to the maître d', who listened to her demand for the police. "He's an impostor and he's out to kill me," said Agatha desperately. "I'll go back and join him but don't alert him."

She went back to the table, a smile pinned on her face. There was another noisy act and she was glad that it was impossible to speak.

In record time, two policemen and one policewoman entered the restaurant. Agatha heaved a sigh of relief as the maître d' pointed at their table.

To Agatha's amazement, the two policemen began to laugh, although the policewoman looked grim.

They all spoke in rapid Turkish and then Mustafa was

led away while the policewoman took his place. "Come outside with me," she said in English.

Agatha followed her out and down the stairs. "There is a café over there where we can talk," she said. "Don't tell them I said anything. I said I would stay behind to comfort you."

"What's it all about?" asked Agatha.

"Who did he say he was?"

"A tax inspector called Mustafa Kemal."

"He is a police inspector from Karakoy, taking a few days' holiday. His name is Demir Oguz and he is married with six children. He is a famous seducer of women. I am sorry. Of course my male colleagues think it is all very funny. What made you call us?"

Agatha wearily told her the story of Sylvan Dubois and the subsequent attempt on her life. She ended by saying, "I don't think I'm any kind of detective at all. I should have recognized his name as fake."

"You are a woman in a foreign country," said the policewoman. "It was an easy mistake to make. Now I will take you back to your hotel."

"Your English is excellent," said Agatha.

"That's why I was brought. When they heard an Englishwoman had called us, they took me with them."

"Why does the police inspector have such good English as well?"

"His wife is from Manchester—poor thing."

• • •

Back in her hotel room, Agatha sank down on the edge of
the bed and eased off her high heels. What a fool she had
been! She remembered the chance meeting with Erol and
how he had turned out to be such a gentleman. Perhaps
that was why she had accepted the invitation from the fake
tax inspector so easily.

Suddenly the idea of giving up detective work flooded
her brain with relief. No more shocks and alarms. No more
nasty divorce cases. She would make Toni, Patrick and
Phil joint owners. She would settle down in the village and
potter about.

She rose to her feet and began to pack. She did not want
to stay any longer in Istanbul in case she ran into whatever
his name was again.

"You're going to do *what?*" demanded Sir Charles Fraith.
Agatha had arrived home to find her friend in residence.

"You heard. I'm fed up with the whole thing."

"But what will you do?"

"I came down to the Cotswolds to retire and that is
exactly what I am going to do now."

"You'll die of boredom. What happened in Istanbul?"

"Nothing."

"But you're back early?"

"The weather turned cold."

Charles studied her face. "Now why do you look exactly like a woman disappointed in love?"

"Stop fantasizing. I am going into the office to break the news to them. It will give me a wonderful feeling of freedom."

"For a couple of days," said Charles cynically.

Agatha called her staff to meet in the office at 5:00 P.M. They were all there when she arrived—Toni, Phil, Patrick, Mrs. Freedman and the two relative newcomers, Paul Kenson and Fred Auster.

She replied briefly to questions about her holiday and then said, "I have decided to retire."

"Why?" asked Toni.

"I need some quality time. You, Toni, Patrick and Phil, will become joint owners. Paul, Fred, Sharon and Mrs. Freedman, you will continue to work as usual."

After the first exclamations of dismay were over, Toni began to feel quite cheerful. She always felt that Agatha was looking over her shoulder. Paul and Fred each privately thought it would be a relief to have bossy Agatha out of the way. Patrick accepted it philosophically. Phil was genuinely distressed. He was in his seventies and felt he owed a lot to Agatha for having hired a man of his age. Thanks to her, he had been able to find a comfortable life with little treats which he could not otherwise have afforded on his pension alone.

"Are you having a retirement party?" asked Toni.

"No," said Agatha. "I'll just leave quietly."

And to their amazement, that is exactly what Agatha did.

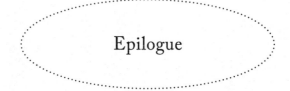

Epilogue

BACK AT HER cottage, Agatha found Charles had left. He had written a message in lipstick on her bathroom mirror: "Big Mistake!" Agatha crossly wiped it off.

She decided to visit Mrs. Bloxby. But the meeting of the Carsely Ladies' Society was in full swing. Agatha blinked in surprise. It was so long now since she had attended a meeting that she barely knew anyone. Particularly with the credit crunch and people unable to pay their mortgages, the population of all Cotswolds villages was shifting and changing. Apart from Miss Simms, Carsely's unmarried mother, and still secretary of the group, it was hard to hear one Gloucestershire accent.

The incomers, from their clothes and accents, were obviously well off. Fresh from the towns, they were all determined to play the part of village ladies—all to the benefit of Mrs. Bloxby, who had new blood to fund her various charities.

Agatha was a celebrity but the newcomers ignored that fact. Each one, with the exception of Miss Simms and Mrs. Bloxby, seemed determined to outdo the others in becoming the leading lady of the village.

I'm one of them now, thought Agatha gloomily, so I may as well make the best of it. But over tea and cakes after a discussion on raising funds for the Red Cross, the women seemed to vie with one another over material possessions. "We're having a sauna," said one, and another chimed in with "We're having a swimming pool put in the old barn." Mrs. Bloxby anxiously studied Agatha's downcast face.

When the meeting was over, Mrs. Bloxby whispered, "Do stay, Mrs. Raisin."

But when the other women saw Agatha settling back in her chair, with the exception of Miss Simms, they all sat down again.

"I'll leave and come back," whispered Agatha.

She went out and walked around the village. Rain was falling steadily and the evening was chilly. Miss Simms tottered beside her on her high heels. "It's not the same at all," she complained. "Lot of toffee-nosed slags. Are you going to walk all night?"

"Maybe," said Agatha.

"Then I'm off."

When Agatha felt she had spent enough time out in the cold, she returned to the vicarage.

"What a shower!" she exclaimed, parking her umbrella in the stand in the hall.

"Shower? It's been raining steadily," said Mrs. Bloxby, helping her off with her coat.

"I didn't mean the weather," grumbled Agatha. "I meant your new members."

"Oh, they'll adjust. Newcomers are always bitten by the village-dream bug," said the vicar's wife. "They'll soon settle down. At the moment, it's very nice for me because they compete in the size of their donations to charity. You are looking quite miserable. What about your holiday?"

"I'll tell you about it," said Agatha, sinking down onto the sofa in the living room, "but if you tell anyone else, I'll have to kill you."

"As bad as that?"

"Worse."

As Agatha told her about the police inspector, Mrs. Bloxby tried hard not to laugh but eventually collapsed into giggles. "You're being a bit cruel," said Agatha huffily.

"Please don't be angry," said Mrs. Bloxby. "I haven't laughed in ages."

"I've given up the detective agency."

"Surely not because of one silly man in Istanbul?"

"It's not that. The Sylvan case finished me. I just blundered around while others showed their intelligence."

"Is Toni the trouble?"

"Why should she be?"

"She's bright and photogenic. You were used before her arrival to always being the one in the newspapers."

"I've lost confidence and I really want to get away from it all."

"But what will you do?"

"Settle down, read, travel, lots of things."

"I could do with your expert help."

"At what?"

"I am planning a charity drive for the local regiment. They are being sent out to Afghanistan and they need lots of things, from paperbacks to shaving cream. I got a whole list from the adjutant."

"What have you done so far?"

"We've put a box outside the village shop for people to leave things."

"Such as?"

"There's a list pinned up. Shaving cream, razors, paperbacks, all sorts of things."

"I'll have a look when I'm next at the shop and see if I can think of something," said Agatha.

·   ·   ·

The next morning Agatha strolled along to the shop. She bought some shaving cream and disposable razors and threw them in the box outside.

"You are Mrs. Raisin, aren't you?" said a male voice behind her. Agatha swung round. A tall man stood looking down at her. He had thick grey hair, glasses and a clever face. "I am new in the village," he said. "May I introduce myself? My name is Bob Jenkins."

Agatha looked up at him warily. The fear that Sylvan might send someone else after her still haunted her. She did not sleep well at nights, thinking every rustle in the thatch was someone on the roof, looking for a way in.

"I hear you are a detective," he said. His voice was warm and pleasant.

"Not any longer," said Agatha. "I've given all that up."

"Why?"

"It's too long a story."

"I am on my way to the Red Lion. They've started serving coffee in the mornings. Care to join me?"

Agatha hesitated. There was nothing sinister-looking about him. Surely nothing could happen to her in her own village and at the local pub.

"All right," she said cautiously.

Seated over coffee in the outdoor smoking section of the pub, Bob told her he had recently moved into the village.

"What brought you to Carsely?" asked Agatha.

"Retirement. I was a schoolteacher for years. I thought it would be marvellous to get away from noisy classes and difficult children. But I find time hanging heavily on my hands. I need a hobby or something."

"Don't you have a wife?" asked Agatha.

"My wife died ten years ago."

"Children?"

"One son in Australia."

"Aren't you tempted to go out and join him?"

"He's married and his wife doesn't like me much. Never mind about all that. Why did you give up detecting?"

Agatha did not want to explain it was because she felt like a failure. She said instead that she had wanted to enjoy some quality time.

"And what will you do?" he asked.

Agatha smiled. "Find a hobby, just like you."

He laughed. "We could fish."

"Boring."

"Hunt?"

"Can't ride."

"Agatha—may I call you Agatha?"

"Please do."

"I feel perhaps neither of us are really country people."

"You're from town?"

"Not London. Manchester. I read about the case of that

Frenchman in the newspapers. That must have been scary. Tell me about it."

So Agatha did, without her usual exaggerations and embellishments.

"How frightening," he said when she had finished. "You must be scared someone else will come after you."

Agatha eyed him narrowly. "Could be you."

"My cottage is full of dreary old photographs of me with various pupils and colleagues. You are welcome to see them anytime. It's a new line when you think of it. Instead of saying, come and see my etchings, I can say, come and see a lot of faded old school photographs. So what do you plan to do with the rest of the day?"

"I'm supposed to be thinking up a fund-raiser for that regiment," said Agatha, "but I can't really get interested in good works."

"You don't need to worry. I was speaking to one of the soldiers who came yesterday to collect the box from the village shop before putting down a new one. The adjutant has arranged a big parade in Mircester with people going around collecting donations. I don't really think you need to bother.

"I know," he said. "We could go into Oxford and take a punt out on the river."

Agatha hesitated. She hadn't had time to check

him out. But the day stretched out before her, long and empty.

"Fine," she said. "You're on."

It was to be the first of many dates. Agatha and Bob seemed to be inseparable. Mrs. Bloxby was anxious and yet could not find any fault in Bob Jenkins, and Agatha looked more relaxed and happy than she could remember ever seeing her.

And then two months after Agatha had first met Bob, she called in at the vicarage with a sparkling diamond ring on her engagement finger.

"So you are really going to get married?" asked Mrs. Bloxby, after Agatha had described the proposal and how happy she was.

"We're really going to see if we suit first," laughed Agatha. "We've taken a self-catering place in Normandy. We're going away for a couple of weeks."

"Do be careful, Mrs. Raisin. It all seems to have happened so fast."

The village of Saint Claire in Normandy was off the beaten track. It was far from the sea and stuck in the middle of acres of farmland.

When they had unpacked their luggage, Agatha asked, "Do you speak French, Bob?"

"Yes, fairly well."

"Good, we'll get in some groceries and find some woman to clean."

"Agatha, that will not be necessary. We can clean the place ourselves."

"Then let's find a café and have something to eat."

He laughed. "We'll find a grocery shop and cook our meals ourselves. I am sure you are a good cook."

"Bob, I have plenty of euros. There is no need to scrimp and save."

"Sit down, my dear, and listen to me. When you are my wife, you will need to do all the things a wife does. So why not start now?"

"Because we're on holiday!" howled Agatha.

"There, now. You're tired after the journey. We'll talk about this later."

"I tell you what," said Agatha desperately, "I'll do the shopping myself. You just relax."

"Can you speak French?"

"I can point at things in English."

Agatha seized her handbag and shot out of the door.

She walked into the village and straight into the central brasserie. It was full of men in working clothes, who all turned and stared at her. She retreated and sat at a table outside and lit a cigarette.

When a waiter came out, she ordered a Calvados and coffee and fretted about Bob. What had come over him? And what was she to do about cooking?

What had his wife died of? Boredom? Why had she plunged into this engagement? Maybe because the women of the ladies' society had been so jealous. Maybe it was because she wanted to prove to herself that she still had pulling power.

When her drink and coffee arrived, she drank them slowly and then went inside to pay for them. Newspapers were hanging up on a rack beside the bar. Sylvan's face stared out at her from one of the front pages.

She took it down and shouted, "Can anyone here speak English?"

A small man came up to her and said in English, "Can I help you?"

Agatha pointed to the writing under Sylvan's photograph. "Can you tell me what this story says?"

He read carefully and then in strongly accented English, he said, "The murderer and smuggler Sylvan Dubois was knifed to death in prison in London. Police are searching for the culprit."

"It's all right," said Agatha breathlessly. "You don't need to read any more."

She paid for her drinks and walked out of the bar, feeling weak with relief. She went to a grocery store and bought bread, cheese, ham and a bottle of wine and carried them back.

Bob looked at her purchases with disfavour. "I like a hot meal," he said.

"Oh, never mind that," cried Agatha. "Sylvan Dubois is dead. It was in a newspaper in the bar."

"This is a small village, Agatha. I don't think it is quite the thing to go into a bar by yourself."

Agatha sat down and studied him. "Bob, what happened to all the fun we had together? Have you drunk something, like Dr. Jekyll, and turned into an old-fashioned household tyrant?"

"This is real life, Agatha. The whole point of coming to this place is to see how we will really get on together once we are married."

"For heaven's sake, Bob, lighten up. Have some bread and cheese, have some wine. We can drive somewhere nice this evening for dinner."

That evening, they drove to the coast and had an excellent meal in a fish restaurant, but Bob's sudden surly mood would not lighten. He refused anything to drink, pointing out that he was driving.

When they got back to the villa they had rented, Bob said curtly that he would sleep in the spare room. Agatha felt hurt and bewildered.

But the following day his mood had turned as sunny as the day outside. Agatha demanded to know what had happened to him and he had said he suffered from headaches. They passed a leisurely day with Bob in high spirits. He seemed inclined to find everything funny and his humour was infectious.

By evening, however, he suddenly said he was tired and would prefer to sleep alone.

"What on earth is up with you now?" demanded Agatha.

"Mind your own business for once in your nosy life!" he said viciously.

She sat alone in the kitchen staring into space. Then she pulled out her mobile and phoned Charles. "How's the married lady?" asked Charles.

"I'm not married and I don't think I'm going to be," whispered Agatha. "He's turned into some sort of old-fashioned household monster. I think he's bipolar or just plain nuts."

"Where are you?"

"In some godforsaken Normandy village called Saint Claire."

"Then get in your car and get the hell out."

"I can't. It's his car."

"Hang on. I'll get there somehow and pick you up. Give me directions to where you are in the village."

"It's the first villa on the north side."

"I'll be there."

"Charles, I love you."

"No, you don't, thank goodness. The thought of the weight of an Agatha obsession terrifies me."

The next day, Agatha wished she had not phoned Charles. Bob was his amusing, relaxing self again. They toured around the countryside, visiting old churches and eating delicious food. Several times, Agatha excused herself and in the privacy of some French toilet tried to phone Charles, without success.

After the last unsuccessful attempt, she went back into the restaurant to join Bob.

"Were you sat there wondering what had become of me?" she asked.

"Agatha, you're a disgrace. The word is *sitting*—get that—sitting. I cannot bear the sloppy use of past participles."

"Okay, don't get your knickers in a twist."

"And you can cut out that vulgarity for a start."

"For goodness' sakes, what's come over you?"

"Nothing has come over me. I dislike bad grammar intensely. For example, the verb is 'sit.' The present tense is 'sit.' The present participle is 'sitting.' The past participle is 'was sitting.' Get it?"

"Don't want it."

"Bad grammar is creeping in all over the place. Do you know that in books, for example, writers now put, say, in the description of a room, 'there were a table and chair,' whereas it should read, 'there was a table and a chair,' the conjunction standing for 'and there was.'"

He really is bonkers, thought Agatha wildly.

"Do you always have these mood swings?" she asked.

"What mood swings?"

"We've been having a very pleasant time up until now."

"If you say so."

"Look, Bob, this is all a big mistake. I don't think we are really suited."

He stood up and walked straight out of the restaurant.

Agatha called the waiter over and asked him to order her a taxi and then paid the bill.

When she got back to the villa, it was in darkness. She tried the front door but it was locked. At that moment, Charles drove up and got out of his car. Agatha threw herself into his arms. "He's locked me out!"

"What about round the back?"

They crept around the side of the building and into the back garden. Agatha tried the kitchen door. "He's forgotten to lock this one. He'll be sleeping in the spare room, and as a precaution I've got most of my things packed."

Fifteen minutes later, Agatha went quietly down the stairs carrying her suitcase. She took off her engagement ring and left it on the table. Then she joined Charles, who was waiting in the car outside.

After several miles, Agatha said, "We're going south."

"So we are. Have a sleep and then take over the driving. We're going to find somewhere sunny and have a fling. Are you on?"

"Yes, I jolly well am," said Agatha.

Toni was worried about the agency. Everyone seemed to be slacking off. At first it had all been very relaxing without the domineering presence of Agatha Raisin around, but now she and Sharon seemed to be doing most of the work themselves. Even Phil and Patrick appeared to have grown lazy.

Now that Agatha was to be married, there seemed to be little hope of her coming back.

They met one Friday for the usual end-of-the-day briefing. Feeling young and inadequate, Toni prepared to rally them by saying they were starting to lose business. She had run her own agency successfully because they had all been young. The two relative newcomers, Paul Kenson and Fred Auster, treated her like a child.

Toni was opening her mouth to deliver another hopeless lecture when the door of the office crashed open and Agatha Raisin walked in. She had a light tan and her eyes were glowing. "I've decided to come back," she said. "Let's get down to business."

•   •   •

Mrs. Bloxby had heard that Agatha had returned home. Bob Jenkins had put his cottage up for sale and had disappeared from the village.

Finally free of demanding parish duties, she called on Agatha one evening.

"Come in," hailed Agatha. "Sherry?"

"Yes, please."

"I've been meaning to call on you sooner. I've brought you some presents from the south of France."

"I thought you were in Normandy."

"I was, until Charles rescued me. Here's your drink. Wait till you hear this."

She told Mrs. Bloxby about Bob's terrifying mood swings and about how Charles had come to rescue her. "So we decided to beetle off to the south of France and have a holiday," said Agatha.

The vicar's wife studied Agatha's glowing face. "You and Charles. You didn't, did you?"

"Didn't what?" said Agatha airily. "I don't know what you're talking about. More sherry?"